A
WOMAN
MISUNDERSTOOD

by
Melinda Clayton

A WOMAN MISUNDERSTOOD

by Melinda Clayton
Copyright 2016 Melinda Clayton

This book is a work of fiction. While some of the place names are real, characters and incidents are the product of the author's imagination and are used fictitiously. Any resemblance to events or persons living or dead is purely coincidental.

Cover fonts: Viper Nora, from FontPalace.com, and Open Sans Light, from 1001Fonts.com.

Title inspiration: *Her Kind*, a poem by Anne Sexton.

ISBN 10: 0-9963884-9-4

ISBN 13: 978-0-9963884-9-8

Library of Congress Control Number: 2016960672
Thomas-Jacob Publishing, LLC Deltona, Florida

First Printing: November, 2016

Published by Thomas-Jacob Publishing, LLC
Deltona, Florida
USA

A false witness shall not be unpunished. He who utters lies shall perish.

Proverbs 19:9

Chapter 1: Rebecca

I ONCE READ that the stench of a decaying human body is similar to that of rotted fish, but that was not my experience. Perhaps it's because I've only witnessed the odor once, or perhaps it's because the one time I did, the number of bodies was multiplied by three and they'd been putrefying for days in the moist heat of a Tennessee summer. Whatever the reasons, it's not an experience I'm likely to forget, not only due to the smell, but also because the corpses were those of my family.

The bodies belonged to my parents and younger sister, the three people in the world for whom I'd been tasked with caring, which is what I'd been trying to do that scorching July morning. I'd pulled into their long, rocky, rutted driveway to perform my usual Saturday chores: mow the lawn, pay the bills, shop for groceries, take my sister out for a treat. It wasn't immediately clear, as I parked under the old pecan tree and stepped out into a wall of heat, that something was wrong. The place looked run down, true, but that had been the case for the past several years, since my father's most recent heart attack.

Forty acres had quickly become too much for him to handle, so he'd rented the farm portion out to another farming family. While the fields had been recently plowed and planted with cotton, the couple of acres surrounding the house were overgrown and neglected. Buttercups grew wild across a lawn filled with Johnson grass, a horrible weed that had killed off our beef cattle years before. Hydrangeas spread shapelessly along the driveway, and the unpruned crepe myrtles hadn't bloomed in years, their scraggly gray branches twisted and turned in a never-ending dance of death.

I did my best to keep the yard in check on the weekends, but given the four-hour drive and my odd work hours, it just wasn't always possible. On a good weekend I managed to get it all mown, which was more than would have happened without me. For years, I'd begged my father to hire someone to help me mow, but he refused, citing cost as the reason. But that wasn't it.

He was a cheap bastard, don't get me wrong. I could probably count on one hand the articles of new clothing I had growing up, and I was the oldest. I doubt my sisters ever saw clothes with store tags still attached. It wasn't for lack of money, either. We had money; we just weren't allowed to spend it. That man could squeeze a penny until it screamed, as my mother used to say.

But that's not why he refused to hire someone to mow his yard. My father grew up in a time in which family cared for family, sons built houses on adjacent acres, and daughters lived at home until they married and went to live in a house built by some other son on some other acre his father had given to him. So that's what he expected of me, even though I'd disappointed in nearly every category, beginning, of course, with my gender. In my father's eyes, son or no, coming home weekends to help was my job, plain and simple.

On that particular morning, it was a little unusual not to see my sister's face plastered against the front window, drool dripping down her chin as she rocked in her wheelchair, squealing with excitement. My visits were the highpoints of Callie's life, sad as that might seem. I suppose compared to every other day, endless days during which Callie sat for hours in front of the T.V., a visit to the local Dairy Queen was pretty exciting, after all.

I'd long ago stopped trying to persuade my parents to enroll Callie in some sort of workshop or day program. When she'd aged out of special education classes at the local high school twenty-eight years prior, that had been the end of Callie's socialization. Family cares for family, my parents would say whenever I brought it up, and so Callie remained at home, living a life that was no sort of life at all.

Of course, that was no longer the case that sweltering summer morning, but it wasn't until I'd climbed the porch steps and opened the front door to that horrible smell that I really began to understand death. When I stumbled over Callie's dead body, my foot slipping and sinking into the rotted flesh of her stomach, I had no choice but to understand.

After I finished screaming, my first thought was to call 911.

My second was to find Lena, my surviving sister.

My third was to wonder how much time we had before her arrest.

This is important, this third thought of mine. If you stick with my story, you'll understand why.

Chapter 2: Rebecca

I WAS BORN on May 3, 1965, the first of three daughters born to Patrick Eugene Reynolds and his lovely wife Becky May. At my mother's insistence, they named me Rebecca, the longer version of her own name, and the one she'd always wanted.

It was no secret my father had wanted a son, nor was it a secret I tried my best to fill the gap. I toddled after him as soon as I was able, riding along on the tractor, gathering eggs, milking cows. I dare say he'd nearly forgotten I was female until puberty hit at the tender age of twelve, at which point he became flustered and curt, shunning my company in the field while reciting a list of daily chores I needed to complete to help my mother care for my younger siblings. It's interesting to me, in my mature years, that when my femininity became obvious, outdoor work was deemed inappropriate, but now that I'm older and surely less fit it's not only appropriate, but expected. One of my father's many idiosyncrasies.

Callie was born in 1969, when I was four years old. I was much too young to understand what was happening at the time, but have since come to understand her disabilities stemmed from a combination of ineptitude and indifference. By all indications, Callie had developed normally in the womb, but when my mother suddenly and unexpectedly went into labor late on a Saturday night, her doctor proved impossible to find.

The nurses in our small-town hospital panicked, literally holding my mother's legs closed until a hospital janitor drove to a bar on the outskirts of town, nearly at the river's edge, to collect the doctor and transport him back to tend to his patient. If you know anything at all about the area of our county called the river bottom, or *the bottoms* for short, you understand the sort of establishment to which I refer. As it turned out, my father was the one who gave the good doctor a ride back to town, the janitor following behind to ensure they made it without taking any side trips into ditches or fence posts.

Make of that what you will.

Mother's legs forced closed equaled pressure on the baby's skull, which equaled pressure on the baby's brain, which equaled brain damage. There you have it. And all so the doctor could drink whiskey and soda in a dump of a bar and ogle barely-legal-aged girls on a Saturday night in the hopes of getting laid, while his social-climbing clueless wife did her best to get laid while drinking cheap chardonnay at the country club on the opposite side of town.

The whole scenario portrays small-town hospitality in a fascinating new light, don't you think?

Anyway, so there was Callie the summer of my twelfth year, the year I was assigned to what my father referred to as *woman's work* back at the house. She was four years younger than I but still in diapers, still unable to speak, sit, or walk. Callie was at the top of my father's list of chores for me to complete. But of course there was no completion; there was just a lifelong, endless cycle of feeding and changing and bathing and pretending all was well in the Reynolds' household, when nothing could have been further from the truth.

Lena, the baby, was at the bottom of the pecking order. How could she have been anywhere else? Lena was born in 1971, two years after Callie, and destined at birth to be the overlooked, forgotten child. Over time, she responded accordingly and gave my parents—and me, by extension—hell. But that was to be expected.

Let me interject here to correct any misconceptions. I realize I may sound bitter, but I'm not. No. I'm a pragmatist. I'll speak openly and honestly about the hand dealt me, without hysterics or emotion, because truly, what's the point? It simply is. Things simply are. So that's the way I'll report it.

I merely want to tell the truth.

Chapter 3: Lena

I WAS IN my therapist's office when the cops showed up. That in and of itself wasn't unusual. I was often in my therapist's office, and I was on a first name basis with the cops. Hell, I was probably closer to the little group crowding into Dr. Lewis' office than I was to anyone else on earth. By close I don't mean close; I mean I could tolerate them, and that's saying something. Seeing them all together wasn't unusual. What was unusual was the way they greeted me. Or more specifically, didn't greet me.

Instead of, "C'mon, Lena, you know why we're here," I got, "Dr. Lewis, we're sorry to interrupt, but we have some disturbing news we need to share with Lena. It might be better if you're present while we talk with her." Dr. Lewis looked at me and raised her brows, and I nodded. What did I care if she heard whatever they wanted to say? The woman already knew I'd started hooking down in the bottoms by the age of sixteen, and first tried to kill a man—unsuccessfully, unfortunately—at the age of seventeen.

They couldn't say anything that would shock Dr. Lewis. Believe me, I'd tried but never succeeded. That was one of the reasons I liked her, when I did.

"Lena, we got a call from your sister this morning. Rebecca."

"Well," I said, drawing out the word. "Thanks for clearing that up for me. For a second there I thought you meant Callie, and that'd have been a miracle, wouldn't it, given how she can't talk."

Officer Frazier—Bill—cleared his throat. "Just listen for a minute, Lena," he said. "This won't be easy."

I had no doubt that was true. Nothing concerning my oldest sister was ever easy. "Look, if this is about that credit card, I already told you—"

"It's not," he interrupted me, and I tensed, ready to give him a piece of my mind. I don't like being interrupted, maybe because I had such a goddamned hard time ever being heard as a kid. Between Righteous Rebecca and Crippled Callie, I was never able to get a word in edgewise.

"Now just settle down," said Bill, knowing where I was headed. We'd had enough encounters over the years we could dang near read each other's minds, by that point. "Lena, honey, this is serious."

Honey? It wasn't the first time he'd called me that, but it was close. Bill had always taken sort of a fatherly approach to me, probably because I was still in Monday panties the first time he arrested me for propositioning an undercover officer. Monday panties—remember those? I wonder if they still make them. Back then, the embroidered underwear was sold in the teen's department of our local Walmart, a seven-pack of panties that covered each day of the week. Mine were hand-me-downs from Rebecca, of course, the Saturday pair missing due to a bout with stomach flu Rebecca had suffered years before I inherited her underwear. I once asked her if she'd really been sick on a Saturday, but she didn't remember, just looked at me as if I were crazy.

Anyway, that's what I was wearing the first time Bill caught me—Monday panties and a flowered sundress, worn thin enough to be translucent. You'd have thought there was enough crime in town to keep our little police force busy away from the bottoms, but no sooner had I reached out my hand for a twenty-dollar bill than Bill came out of the bushes along the riverbank and slapped the cuffs on. My wrists were so skinny back then he'd used one cuff for me, and engaged the double lock on the other to keep me from snaring him, his buddy, or anyone else I could reach. I couldn't trap them, but I did my best to create havoc by slinging that extra cuff around. By my second arrest, he'd gotten smart enough to clip the loose cuff to the one around my wrists.

He'd lectured me all the way back to the station about how I was ruining my life—a joke if ever there was one, since I didn't have much of a life to ruin—and I'd sat quietly and put up with it because I was too close to tears to argue back. It wasn't getting arrested that started me bawling; I didn't care about that. I knew I'd be given food and a cot, which was more than I had at my little campsite down by the river. No, it was because someone cared enough to lecture me.

Or maybe he didn't. Maybe that wasn't it at all. I suppose when you're arresting the daughter of the town mayor, it pays to be nice. Either way, whatever the reason, he'd always treated me well, and I appreciated that.

Whether it was his use of the term of endearment or the building tension in the room, I can't say, but for whatever reason, I ran out of steam before I even got started. Slouching back down in my chair, I motioned impatiently for him to continue. "But sit down, would you, Bill? Y'all make me nervous standing over me that way."

He sat on the edge of the chair across from me, his duty belt creaking with the movement, and removed his hat, swiping the top of his bald head with a handkerchief. I was surprised to see him looking nervous; he was usually the blustery sort, loud, obnoxious. Not unkind, just sure of himself. His partner, a young guy I hadn't yet met and assumed was in training—as the old guy, Bill always got stuck training the newbies—leaned against the wall and stared at the floor.

No eye contact. Interesting. The young bucks usually like to try to stare me down. I think they're afraid of me, terrified I might tempt them, or maybe shame them. I've never hidden my sexual appetite, and I refuse to change my ways just because some little pansy doesn't know how to handle it. Or maybe they just know I don't give a shit what they think, and that makes them angry. Whatever the reason, not a one of them has ever succeeded in our little staring contests. All their bravado and swagger is horseshit. I know it, and so do they, when I'm finished with them. Sometimes I think Bill brings the young ones by me so he can see if they'll break. They usually do.

But that little boy, he stared at the floor and fidgeted with his belt. That alone made me curious. I slipped the strap of my tank top off one shoulder and edged the scooped neck down to the swell of my breasts. When that didn't get his attention, I let my knees fall apart and ran one long, red nail up my inner thigh to the hem of my shorts. The raspy sound of nail on skin was loud in the crowded space, but I have to hand it to the kid; he never raised his eyes. His studious attention to Dr. Lewis' carpet tickled me, and I allowed myself a chuckle.

From her chair behind the desk, Dr. Lewis sighed, and I shot her a grin. I could almost hear what she was thinking. *Defense mechanisms, Lena. What's making you so defensive right now?* I knew this because Dr. Lewis is big on defense mechanisms, and sometimes she's right. I have all kinds of ways to keep myself protected from people who might want to do me harm. None of my ways are healthy, as Dr. Lewis would say, but all of them are effective, and that's what counts.

Sometimes Dr. Lewis is wrong, although she would argue with me about that. Sometimes my actions have nothing to do with protecting myself and everything to do with hurting somebody else, not because they've done anything to me, but because I just generally hate the world and every asshole in it. I have an arsenal full of ways to make people miserable—fucking with the minds of young cops, for example—and as they say, I'm not afraid to use it. In fact, some days I relish the opportunity.

Dr. Lewis thinks I'm bluffing. She insists somewhere underneath it all is a scared little girl. *All that anger is just masking the hurt*, she says. It's a nice sentiment, but the sad little girl disappeared a long time ago. Dr. Lewis is afraid to accept the truth about me.

If there's no broken-hearted little girl hidden inside making me act the way I do, then what's wrong with me? That's a question Dr. Lewis doesn't want to have to answer. I know her just as well as she knows me.

"We've been out to your house this morning," Bill was saying, which of course means my parents' house, since I don't have one. "Something terrible has happened, Lena. Your mom and dad, Callie … They didn't make it."

"What do you mean didn't make it? Spit it out, Bill." God Almighty, I hate it when people talk all around an issue. Man up, for heaven's sake. Grow some balls. "You mean they're dead? If that's what you mean, say it."

He nodded. "That's what I mean, Lena. They're dead. Murdered."

The three of them were staring at me, waiting to see my reaction. I don't know what they were expecting. Tears? Hysterics? Whatever it was, I didn't give it to them, and for once it wasn't because I was messing with their heads.

It was because I honestly didn't give a damn.

Chapter 4: Rebecca

SOME DAYS, I just sit and cry. I've been that way all my life. "You never have been happy," my mother used to say, "and you never will be."

This announcement didn't require any sort of special knowledge on her part, no second sight. I had nothing to be happy *about*; that was easy enough for anyone with half a brain to see. Look, I've seen the same social media memes you've seen. I know I'm supposed to talk about the privilege of caring for someone with disabilities. I'm supposed to frame everything in a soft lens and accompany it with a swell of orchestral music while I assure people that the birth of Callie has been a blessing in my life.

That stuff really pisses me off, you know? What do the people posting those memes and verses and inspirational quotes know about anything? Tell me that. Nothing, that's what. It's too damn easy to sit behind the anonymity of a keyboard and tell everyone else how they should feel about the challenges in their own fucking lives.

It's true there are times I enjoy Callie. She loves me unconditionally, and God knows that's a blessing; she's the only one who ever has. She's also the one person who's always happy to see me, my own little welcoming committee complete with soiled diapers and crusty teeth. Callie never greets me with a litany of complaints, a manipulative guilt trip, or, in the case of my sister Lena, a grab for my money. Callie greets me with outstretched arms and a goofy grin.

But let's not pretend that makes up for everything. I love Callie, in my own way, but the truth of the matter is it's because of Callie I have to live within commuting distance of the suffocating little house in which I grew up. It's because of Callie that I never went to college. Callie is the reason I work at a dead-end job that has nothing to do with anything in which I've ever been even remotely interested. How many people do you know who're passionate about factory work? Filling boxes with rivets for hours on end was certainly never a dream of mine.

Callie is also the reason I never married, and the reason I have no children.

She's the reason I lost the love of my life.

I suppose I could spread some of the blame among my parents and Lena, since they too have become my responsibility, but really, when you get down to it, that's also because of Callie. Her existence changed the dynamics of my family. Over the years, I watched my parents withdraw from outside social activities and completely immerse themselves in The World According to Callie. Any meaningful discussion of outside events, whether of politics, religion, or the construction of the new Kroger on the far side of town, was replaced with whether she might have sat up *just a little bit* on her own that morning as my mother was strapping her into the wheelchair, or maybe, just *maybe*, she had said *Daddy* when he walked through the door after a late night city council meeting.

More often, Lena and I were treated to a daily tally of the frequency and consistency of Callie's bowel movements, or which doctor said what, and whose turn it was to pick up her dozens of prescriptions from the pharmacy.

Eugene, does she feel clammy to you?

Maybe a little. Has she taken a shit today?

Just one, and it wasn't a big one. Little pellets, hard ones, like rabbit poop. I think she's constipated.

What do you want me to do about it? Stick my finger up there to find out? We have enemas if she needs one.

And on, and on, and on, while I scraped my plate into the garbage can, no longer hungry, and wet a dishrag to clean up the floor under Lena's highchair.

That was the world into which Lena was born; she can hardly be blamed for turning out the way she did. It wasn't so much that Lena was hard to find, lost as she was in the shadow of Callie, as it was that her presence was completely *obliterated* by Callie. Looking back, I have very few memories of Lena as she was before hightailing it down to the bottoms to take up residence with the pimps and drug dealers. It's a sad commentary on her life, and ours as well, that she found their company more desirable than ours, but I understand it. I do.

Still, Lena's choices have added to my burden. I'm the one who has to beg Mr. Calhoun down at the Shell station not to press charges when Lena bounces checks—*stolen* checks, to be clear. I'm also the one they call when Lena gets thrown into jail for public drunkenness, or when First Baptist Church discovers—not for the first time, or even the third—the money from Sunday's collection has been swiped right out of the locked pantry in the church basement before Miss Trudy even has a chance to get it to the bank.

These are the events that make up my life. They're the reason some days I just sit and cry, which is exactly what I was doing in the little interrogation room they put me in at the police station. I sat on that hard wooden chair, one I could have sworn, given the carvings, had at some point been part of the décor in my third grade classroom down at Hemmings Elementary School, and cried the same, hiccup-y sobs I'd cried out at the house when the police cruisers finally pulled up.

"Let's get you out of here," the policewoman had said, taking me by the arm as soon as she exited the first car. She was a brusque, dark-skinned woman I vaguely recognized from past trips to the station to deal with Lena. She was quick and efficient, and I supposed that may have been why she was assigned to me instead of crouching down with the other officers and creeping towards the front porch as if my mother might have reattached her head and taken up residence behind the front door, waiting to ambush them. "We need to mark off the area," the woman was saying, "and you don't need to be here to see this."

It was a little late for that, since I still had remnants of what I assumed to be Callie's intestines on my shoe, but I didn't argue. "You're not under arrest, honey," she said. "You know that. But since you're the one who made the call, we need to get some information from you. Understand?"

I nodded, and she nodded back. "Follow me back to the station, if you would. Where's your sister at?" she asked. "Do you know? We'll need to talk with her, too."

I didn't know where Lena was, and even if I had, I wouldn't have told the cops. I'd been born and raised to protect, after all. If the evidence pointed to Lena, and I assumed it would, they'd figure that out soon enough. I wasn't going to help them. The woman nodded again before situating her considerable bulk back into her own driver's seat and leading me three pothole-filled, soybean-surrounded, country-laned miles to the squat, one-story building out on Highway 51 that houses the handful of officers making up Owensfield's police department.

I don't know how long I'd been in that freezing little room, wiping snot on my shirttail and curling into the hard wood of my chair for warmth, before I heard Lena's voice, argumentative and angry, and knew they'd managed to find her. Her words faded as someone, Bill Frazier, it sounded like, propelled her down the hall to the staff lounge, which I knew from previous visits doubled as another interrogation room on the rare occasion they needed a second one.

As crazy as it might sound—which probably isn't any crazier than the rest of this sorry story—a part of me felt comforted knowing my sister was there with me, even though I couldn't see her. She certainly didn't love me, didn't even like me, but she was all I had left. I felt relatively sure she'd eventually be arrested for the murder of our family. I didn't know quite how to feel about that yet—sad? sorry? grateful?—but what I did feel at that moment was a warmth towards my sister, a nostalgic sort of longing for what should have always been, but never was.

Chapter 5: Lena

WHERE'VE YOU BEEN for the last week, they want to know. How's your relationship with your parents? With your sister? Of course, they phrased it all as if they were simply concerned about me, but it didn't take long for me to figure out where they were going with it.

Some of their questions were easier to answer than others. As for where I'd been for the last week, well ... I spent Tuesday recuperating from a bad trip I'd taken thanks to Willie G, a toothless old bastard who billed himself as one of the more experimental drug dealers down in the bottoms. I don't know what he shot into the top of my hand, but it caused one hell of a trip. My last memory, before coming to half-naked along the riverbank, was of running into Willie G. when I had no money in my pocket and a hungry gnawing in my belly.

"I got something for you," he'd said, and for the longest time, I ignored him. Willie G. always had something for somebody, but he didn't have what I needed, which was food. Finally, after I'd walked a good mile through the cockleburs and cattails that grew along the muddy banks, I turned to him.

"What is it, G.? Anything that'll keep my belly from eating away at my backbone?" I'd given up my search by then, the empty fast food wrappers and plastic bottles that always lined the bank curiously empty of the food scraps and watery drinks of Co-Cola they usually harbored. I almost always found soggy chicken nuggets or moldy bread or even rank-smelling burger patties, but that day there'd been nothing. Even Patty Sue, the fat old woman with ratty gray hair hanging in clumps down her back, who lived in half of a rusted out trailer back in the woods, Patty Sue with a heart of gold but an empty head who sometimes brought fried apple pies down to the river and prayed over our poor lost souls as we gobbled up those pies, even she hadn't made an appearance that day.

So there I was. "Whaddaya got, G.?" Maybe whatever it was would take the edge off my hunger.

What he'd had was something that knocked me out for an entire day. I remember shooting up on Monday and waking up on Tuesday with one hell of a headache and a mouth dryer than the dust in old Timmy Tate's cornfields after a month of summer drought. At least I was no longer hungry.

Wednesday and Thursday were easier to remember. I'd spent those days earning a hundred bucks and God only knows what STDs from one of Owensfield's finest men in blue. I can only surmise Owensfield's other men in blue decided there was no reason to ask about Wednesday and Thursday, since the questioning took a quick turn towards my relationships with family, safer territory for them, no doubt, but not so much for me.

"I'm so sorry about your loss, Lena." Bill set a cup of coffee in front of me. I hadn't seen him since he'd led me down the hall, but at his appearance the other officers stood and quietly left us alone, closing the door on their way out. "When's the last time you saw your family?"

"Don't know."

"Days? Weeks? Months?"

"Don't know. Years, maybe. Probably."

"When's the last time you saw Rebecca?"

That was easy. "About a month ago. When I stole her credit card. I did steal it, you know. It was nice of her to drop the charges, though."

"Lena, I'm trying to help you, here."

"What do you want me to say? I don't know the last time I saw my family, and you already know about Rebecca's card. It's been a long time since I've seen the rest of them. Family dinners just haven't been as cozy since Daddy disowned me back around ninety-three, right after I showed up stoned at the Miss Teen Soybean Pageant."

It was true; he'd disowned me right then and there, his twangy voice making the declaration loudly enough to be heard over the sound of the squealing microphone he held in his hand. I don't know what upset him more, the fact that I was stoned and topless when I stumbled up on stage, or the fact that I turned to the stupidly hopeful Miss Teen Soybeans arranged like so many colorful flower stalks behind him and told them to run while they still could. I thought it was damned good advice, myself, but apparently he didn't agree.

"You hated your parents, didn't you, Lena?"

I could see Bill wasn't going to give up anytime soon. "Yes, I did," I told him. There wasn't any point in lying about it. "What wasn't to hate? You know how it was, Bill. You worked side by side with him in the early days on the beat, before he went over to the county. Did *you* like him?" He ignored the question, but I knew the answer. "Of course I hated them. This isn't news to you or to anyone else in town."

"I hear he softened up some after he retired."

"A soft piece of shit is still a piece of shit," I responded, and Bill rubbed a hand over his face before continuing.

"Did you kill them?"

"You haven't read me my rights," I said. "Shame on you, Bill."

"You're not under arrest."

"Bad form, to ask a question like that." I lit a cigarette, ignoring the *No Smoking* signs plastered around the room, coaxing the cherry along. I had no idea how old the butt was or how long it'd been in the pocket of my shorts. It was damp with my sweat, but it finally took, and I filled my lungs with smoke.

"Don't you watch T.V. Bill? Hell, every other show is a crime show. That's all y'all have on in the dayroom when I check into Owensfield's self-locking, one-way motel." I took another drag, doing my best to annoy him. If it was working, he didn't show it. "I never have understood that," I said, flicking ashes on the floor. "Showing televised crime shows to criminals. *CSI*, *Criminal Minds*, that shit. Granted, they're on all the time, but still. Is it because y'all are hoping to learn something from them?"

He didn't answer, just continued to watch me.

"Never mind; don't answer that." I was getting bored with the game. After so many years, he was very nearly an expert at not reacting to me. "My point is, even I know if I said yes, it wouldn't be admissible in court."

"I was hoping we could talk more as friends," he said, his expression unreadable. "Nothing formal."

"Nothing formal, eh?" I exhaled loudly, his face temporarily lost in the gray swirl of smoke. "You're wearing blue, Bill. Take off your uniform, and then we'll be friends." I winked and blew him a kiss, causing him to turn away briefly, a flush spreading up his cheeks. Finally, a reaction, as I'd known there would be. It was a cheap shot. Sexual propositions from me had always been Bill's weak spot, a nearly guaranteed way to get him to blush. It was so easy, and made him so uncomfortable, I almost felt bad about it. I'd taken the cheap way out. I could do better, but not that day. That day, I was ready to get on the road, back to the safety of the pimps and drug dealers with whom I shared the bottoms.

"Lena, if you did this," he said turning back to me, "we'll find out soon enough. Is there anything you want to tell me?"

I shook my head, eager to get the interview over with and be on my way. "No. Not that I can remember. When did it happen, do you know yet? The beginning of the week was kind of a blur for me."

"I don't have the official word yet, but with the heat, given the evident putrefaction—"

"Too much information." I held up my hand. I'd hated my family, but that didn't mean I wanted to hear all the gory details of their deaths. "Just give me a timeline."

"Several days ago," said Bill. "About the time you claim you were blacked out."

"You were watching them question me," I said, looking towards the one-way mirror on the wall.

He shrugged. "Part of the job." So much for informal. "My best guess is they were killed Monday night, maybe before sunrise Tuesday morning, but that's the medical examiner's call. He might come up with something different, but I'd bet money it was no later than that."

I turned that nugget of information over in my mind. Could I have killed them? Emotionally, morally, I probably could have. It's a terrible thing to admit about oneself, but there it is. Physically, though, I wasn't so sure. I still looked good for my age, but I wasn't in the best of shape. "How'd they die?" I asked, realizing I didn't yet know, and wondering why I'd assumed it must have taken physical strength.

"You haven't heard?" Bill looked at me slant-eyed.

"Who the hell would I have heard from? I've been with you and your fellow boy scouts since I found out they were dead, and none of y'all have seen fit to share that information with me."

He shrugged. "Didn't die pretty," he said. "Let's just leave it at that, for now."

I shrugged right back at him. "Well, they didn't live pretty, either, so I guess that's fitting."

He frowned. "Lena, you're not helping yourself."

I smashed my cigarette out on the table and shoved my chair back, impatient with Bill and his not-so-subtle suggestions. Why, after all these years, would I have gone to my parents' home to begin with? Under no circumstances, stoned or otherwise, could I imagine setting foot in that house.

"Am I under arrest?"

Bill looked me up and down, his gaze lingering on my hands and arms, and I was suddenly self-conscious, remembering the scratches and bruises, wounds I'd paid little attention to upon waking alongside the riverbank, wounds which had no doubt been caused by my scavenging for food, but which now ....

"You're here voluntarily, Lena," Bill was saying. "But if you have any unfinished business you need to attend to, I'd suggest you get it done sooner rather than later." He stood, and I stood with him. "Might not be a bad idea to be thinking about an attorney." He hesitated for a second before reaching into his shirt pocket and dropping a business card on the table.

I leaned over to take a look, the foiled lettering of the card reflecting the harsh fluorescent lights and momentarily obscuring the words. "Brian Stone," I read, picking up the heavy, gilt-edged cardstock. "Fancy. Who is he?"

"The best there is," said Bill. "At least he used to be. Not sure now. Ran into some personal trouble a couple of years ago after a tough case. But he's the one I'd call first, if I needed somebody. By the way, Rebecca's here," he said, quickly changing the topic, "if you want to see her."

"Is she a suspect, too?" I asked, slipping the card into the back pocket of my shorts. "Wait, let me guess. Of course she's not a suspect, because she's Rebecca, the responsible one. Am I right?"

"Everyone is a suspect," he answered, then held the door open and motioned me towards the lobby, where Rebecca stood looking like a devastated, healthier, older version of me. For just an instant, my heart ached, but then it passed.

Chapter 6: Lena

I WOULDN'T SAY Rebecca was exactly pleased to see me. I certainly wasn't met with hugs and kisses, but she did fall into step beside me as I made my way to her car, which I took as a good sign. I had no idea where she was going, but I hoped food would come into play somewhere along the line.

"Now what?" I asked, as she unlocked the doors and I slid into the passenger seat.

She looked at me almost as if she didn't recognize me at first, then glanced down at her shoes. "I don't know," she said. "I have to wash. I need new clothes. Oh, God, Lena." She covered her face with her hands.

"Look," I said, "before you have a nervous breakdown, start the car and turn on the air conditioner. You stink." I wrinkled my nose against the awful odor emanating from my sister.

She startled, then sat up and turned the key, not only cranking the air conditioner all the way up, but rolling down the windows, as well. "It's not me," she said. "It's Callie." Then she barked a harsh laugh before shoving open the car door and puking up whatever contents she'd had in her stomach, with a few extra heaves thrown in for good measure.

I didn't know what she meant, and an innate self-preservation dictated I not ask. Instead, I sat quietly until she finished, then watched as she kicked her shoes off, leaving them on the blacktop of the parking lot before she slammed her door shut.

"Hey, I could use those shoes!" People never seem to see the value in the things they have. I could have worn them, bartered them, or sold them. Her careless disregard pissed me off.

"Trust me. You don't want them."

I turned to stare out the window. The day was hot and humid, the sort of day in which you see phantom puddles and snakes on the hot asphalt, but as you get closer they shimmer into nothingness. A *mirage*, my fifth grade teacher had said. *Something that appears real, but isn't.* You don't have to be in the desert to see a mirage.

Hell, by the age of ten I was well acquainted with that one. My whole *life* was a mirage. I wasn't what you'd necessarily call a gifted child, but that I knew. *Smile*, Daddy would say. *Goddamn it, girl, smile! The people are watching.* And he'd straighten my *Vote for Eugene* hat, pinch me—hard enough to leave a bruise—on the back of my arm, and then turn and smile for Benny Young, the photographer for the local newspaper.

So I'd smile, holding back the tears, not so much upset at the angry words he'd sprayed at me, or even the pinch, but at the hypocrisy of it all. We dressed in nice clothes, hosted dinners, donated to charities, and doled out soup at the local soup kitchen. We had our picture in the paper more times than I can count, always smiling, joshing, and hugging, the epitome of a happy, healthy, all-American family. But none of it was real.

We hated each other. Wait. Perhaps I misspeak. *I* hated *them*, but maybe a more accurate description of what they felt would be *apathy*. They just didn't *care*, which I've come to believe, in its own way, is even worse than hate. I think over time my parents came to hate me, too, but that was because I was the only one ballsy enough to call a spade a spade. Loudly, and in public, which brought me great pleasure but no doubt raised my father's blood pressure a few dozen points. They *needed* Rebecca, so she escaped the worst manifestations of their unhappiness, but they *didn't* need me, so I took the full force of their anger.

"Where are we going?" Rebecca was asking, drawing my attention away from my memories.

"You're asking me?" I said, turning to face her. She looked like hell, and smelled like Jones Creek after our small town's septic drain fields had failed.

"Lena," she said, hitting the steering wheel. "Lena, Lena, Lena." She dropped her head onto the wheel, swerving dangerously close to the ditch.

"Whoa, girl, get a grip," I yelled, yanking her head up by the hair and grabbing the wheel. "Pull over," I ordered. "Now, before you kill us."

She obeyed, swinging the wheel to the right too quickly, causing the tires to squall, and wresting the car into the parking lot of Barb's Country Cooking.

"What the hell is wrong with you?" I asked, as soon as she'd put the car in park.

"What's *wrong* with me?" She looked at me, her eyes wide. "I just literally stumbled over the body of our dead sister. Do I need a better excuse than that?"

I didn't answer her right away. What could I say? I wouldn't mourn the death of my family; there was nothing to mourn. If I'd ever had any sadness, and I was sure I must have at some point, it had ended years, if not decades, before. Still, although Rebecca and I were little more than strangers, I had enough sense to realize she was struggling, and I had no desire to make it harder for her. We sat in silence for several moments.

"Did they ask you if you'd killed them?" I finally asked.

"No!" She turned to me in apparent disbelief. "Of course not. Did they ask you?"

It might have been my imagination, but I could have sworn I detected a slight change in her demeanor with the question, a drawing back, a closing up.

"Frazier did," I admitted. "But Becca, I didn't do it. You know that. I haven't been in that house in years. They didn't even exist to me. There was no reason for me to kill them."

She stared ahead, watching a family of four exiting the restaurant. A dad, mom, toddler, baby. I wondered if the scene affected her the way it did me. I hated the family on sight.

"I have to go home," she said. "I need … I don't know what I need. I need to shower, for one thing. And I'm supposed to work tonight, filling in for Brenda. She's on vacation, and I said … but I don't know if I can …" She trailed off.

"Bill suggested I get a lawyer," I said, reaching to my pocket and pulling out the card. "Sooner rather than later, he said."

Rebecca turned to study me again, and I could almost hear her thoughts. *Again, Lena? Why do I have to be saddled with you?* But she didn't say anything, so neither did I. Instead, I opened my door. "So I'd better let you go," I said, resigning myself to the fact there was no food to be had in our brief encounter.

"Can I take you somewhere?" she asked. "To the bottoms? Where are you staying now?"

I shook my head. "Nowhere," I answered, "and I can get there on my own." I stood and moved to close my door, but she reached out a hand to stop me.

"We'll take care of this, Lena. We'll get you a lawyer, okay?"

I bent down to get a closer look at her face. She looked sincere. Hell, she looked *worried*. "How're we going to afford a lawyer, Rebecca? Neither of us is exactly rolling in dough."

"The estate," she said, and then started bawling again. "God, it feels horrible to already be thinking about what to do with the house, the farm." She sat back, wiping her nose on her palm. "But that's what Mom and Dad would want us to do, so that's what we're going to do."

I doubted very much that was what Mom and Dad would have wanted us to do. I doubted very much they'd have given a single shit about what happened to either of us, but I kept my thoughts to myself and handed her the attorney's card. "This is the card Bill gave me. Said he's the best, or was, anyway, until he flaked out over something a couple of years ago."

"Wonderful," Rebecca muttered, before tucking it into the side pocket of her purse. "I'll call him, Lena. Just let me get myself together, figure out where I'm going. Figure out … oh, God, I don't even know. But I'll give him a call, I swear. Where can I find you?"

"Your guess is as good as mine," I said. I closed the door and she took off for the highway, accelerating from the lot and heading north. I started walking south, sticking out a thumb when anyone passed by going in my direction. Someone would stop, eventually. They always did. Not without expectations, mind you, but I'd get to where I was going, and maybe with a little something to show for it.

Hiraeth. The word came from nowhere, bringing with it a foggy memory. My fifth grade teacher again, wearing purple and holding a nub of yellow chalk in her right hand. We'd been reading Barrie's *Peter Pan*, I remembered. *A feeling of homesickness,* she'd said, *for a place to which you can't go back, or maybe even for a place you've never been. What does that mean to you? Write three paragraphs …"*

I understood the meaning even then, and to my surprise, I was hit with it afresh as I walked into the distance alone.

Chapter 7: Brian Stone

I WAS ASLEEP when the phone rang. I realize conventional wisdom says not to start a story that way—overdone, they say—but isn't that the way it so often happens? Besides, I've never been a fan of convention. So, I was asleep. Or passed out. Choose whichever suits you; it hardly matters. At any rate, the damn phone woke me up.

I didn't recognize the number on the screen, and I very nearly didn't answer it. Even now, I'm not sure why I did. The thrill of the unknown, maybe. The lingering, muddled effects of alcohol, more likely.

"What?" I'm not my best when hung over.

"Um. Oh. I was trying to reach Mr. Stone, the attorney?" The voice was hesitant, which for whatever reason, only served to annoy me.

"You did," I responded, "and I'm quite busy." A blatant lie, unless scratching one's nether regions constituted busyness, and I supposed, if push came to shove, it did. "What can I do for you?" Even in my disheveled state, I felt it important to keep up appearances, and the specter of a drunk, naked, unshaved middle-aged attorney who's seen better days wasn't exactly the appearance I needed to uphold.

"I need an attorney," the disembodied voice said. "Or rather, my sister does. We were given your name."

"Why do you need an attorney, and by whom were you given my name?" I sat up, disentangling myself from bedcovers long past their original colors. The room spun, and I stunk. Vaguely, I wondered when I'd last bathed. I surreptitiously sniffed at my armpit as if the woman on the other end of the line might smell me.

"By Bill Frazier. And because he thinks my sister murdered my family."

I had to admit, that was an interesting conversation starter.

"Mrs.—? Miss—?"

"Ms. But just call me Rebecca. Rebecca Reynolds."

"Okay. Ms. Rebecca Reynolds, did Bill Frazier also tell you I'm semi-retired?"

A pause. Then, "No. He told me—or rather, he told my sister, the one suspected of killing my family—you'd flaked out after some sort of personal involvement in a case. I'm hoping you aren't so vagarious as to be unhelpful."

Vagarious. Not an altogether uncommon word, but uncommonly used. Her use of it piqued my interest. I've long been a lover of language. I sighed, standing to get a glimpse of myself in the full-sized mirror attached to my closet door. *Old*, I thought. *Tired, and old. And saggy. Saggy* was a new one.

"I suppose you want to meet with me," I said, still cranky in spite of my intrigue. I hadn't accepted a new case in nearly two years, and I was rusty. Still, I needed the money and this case sounded more interesting than the typical drug-bust-slash-robbery stuff that usually crossed my desk. Or that *had* crossed my desk. I couldn't say what currently crossed it, as I hadn't sat at it in weeks, not since cutting a deal for the spoiled teenaged son of a wealthy local business owner.

He was the last of my caseload. For just over two years, I'd worked methodically through case after case with the intention of walking out when I got to the end. Raymond Ghallagher Junior accepted a hefty fine, which he could well afford to pay, along with probation and community service for the petulant boy slouching in my office chair—Raymond Ghallagher the Third—and the deal was done.

It was fair; I hadn't liked the boy with his ever-present earbuds and cellphone, but I also didn't think he was a lost cause. A year in what the kid had called "juvie" for what amounted to a bit of criminal mischief would surely do more harm than good, if for no other reason than that it would go a long way towards solidifying the kid's belief that the criminal justice system was rigged against young men of color. While in some places that might be true—hell it *is* true, and we all know it—I intended to prove to him that that wasn't the case on *my* watch. If he appreciated my efforts he didn't show it, just continued to slump and stare at his phone while his dad shook my hand, but at least *I* could rest easy.

It was a good case on which to end my career, but truth be told, I'd spent so much time planning to quit I hadn't put any time into planning what I might do afterwards, and with nothing to anchor me, *afterwards* was turning out to be a really bad idea. Too much idle time has never been good for me.

"I'd appreciate it," Ms. Rebecca Reynolds was saying, and for an instant, lost in thought, I had to remind myself of her call. "Does my sister need to be there? I ask because she has a rather"—she paused, before resuming—"unusual lifestyle. She may be difficult to find."

This was sounding more interesting by the second. "If she's to be my client," I said, pacing to the front window of my condo and staring out at the twilit Memphis evening (how long had I slept, anyway?), "her presence is rather necessary."

"I'll find her," she said, her tone no longer hesitant. "When can you meet with us?"

Anytime, I could have said, given my appointment calendar was empty. Instead, I made a show of hemming and hawing before finally offering, "Wednesday. I've had a cancellation at two o'clock. Will that work? It's the soonest I have. Otherwise, it could be weeks." I inwardly cringed at the lie. Contrary to the belief that attorneys exist by lying, I always tried to tell the truth. Often failed, but always tried.

She quickly agreed, and I supplied directions to an office I'd loathed since learning my best friend had killed his wife. I clicked the phone off and stood with my forehead pressed against the steamed glass of the tenth story window. Below me, cars zipped around the busy streets, just beginning to turn on headlights as the day faded to dusk. I didn't want to see clients. I didn't want to do anything other than leave, abdicate, renounce. I disappointed myself with my inability to think of a better word. More interesting synonyms aside, I accepted that the universe wasn't assisting me with my ultimate goal, and closed the blinds. I switched on the desk lamp and logged onto my computer to see what I could find out about Ms. Rebecca Reynolds and her unusual-lifestyle sister.

Chapter 8: Rebecca

I HUNG UP from talking with the attorney and sat with a sigh, the lumpy back of the hotel's chair pressing into my kidneys.

I'd driven for an hour before I'd had to pull over somewhere just past Jackson to rent a room for the night. I was in no shape to drive the three more hours needed to take me home to Kentucky.

Pulling into the lot of a low-slung, nondescript motel, I'd scrolled to Brenda's number on my cell and left a message letting her know I wouldn't be able to fill her shift. Next, I'd called my supervisor and told him I needed the week off.

At first he'd laughed. "Don't we all," he said, "but that's too bad. You're supposed to fill in for Brenda tonight; I can't find anyone else on such short notice."

"Well, I'm afraid you're going to have to," I'd said, "because my family has been murdered." The end of my sentence landed on a decidedly hysterical note, my voice spiraling up and cracking at the end.

"Damn, Rebecca. Are you serious?" His tone had gone from irritated to concerned.

"'Fraid so," I'd managed to choke out, before once again dissolving into sobs.

"Take the week," he'd said. "Don't worry about it; we'll handle it. And Rebecca?"

"What?"

"Let me know if I can do anything, okay? Anything at all."

"I appreciate it," I'd said, clicking off before I lost even more control of my emotions. Kindness always did me in.

The place was a dump, but that suited me fine. I was in desperate need of a hot shower and a deep, dreamless sleep. Besides, not just any place will let you rent a room when you show up barefoot, looking and smelling as if you'd just crawled out of Jones Creek. I'd used my credit card to check in, grateful it wasn't completely maxed out, then inquired as to the nearest clothing store. I couldn't fathom putting my soiled clothes back on; I hoped to never see them again.

"K-Mart is right across the street, in that strip mall," the clerk had said, eying me in a way that at any other time I might have found offensive. She tucked a strand of lank brown hair behind one ear and popped her gum. "But Ma'am, I don't think they'll let you in without shoes." I'd glanced down at my feet, as if needing confirmation that I was, indeed, barefoot.

"Look here," she'd said, snapping her fingers. "I've got some old flip-flops in my car. You can use them. You know what? Just keep them," she'd said, wrinkling her nose. "I don't wear them anymore." She walked from behind the counter, brushing past me with a hugely pregnant belly, and motioned me to follow her to the parking lot, where the late afternoon blacktop was so hot I'd had to hop from foot to foot while I waited for her to open the trunk.

"Here you go," she'd said, handing me a pair of flip-flops nearly worn through, the original blue of the soles black from use. I took them gratefully, slipping them on with relief. "Go ahead and take your key," she'd said, handing it to me. "That way you can just go straight to your room when you get back."

I wasn't sure if she was being thoughtful, or if she just didn't want me gracing the hotel lobby with my presence, but I supposed it didn't matter either way. Taking the key, I'd turned and headed across the busy four-lane highway to the local K-Mart, where I bought a set of undergarments and a bright purple tracksuit, not my style, but better than what I had. After all, I only had to make it through the night before I could get home and figure out what I needed to do.

Bill had told me there would be autopsies, which didn't make sense to me because it seemed obvious, given my quick glance, what the manner of death had been. But he said that was mandatory with any homicide in Tennessee. "And besides," he'd said, "we'll learn a lot from the exam: time of death, weapons used, possibly even something significant like hairs or threads left behind by the perpetrator."

When the autopsies were completed, the bodies would be released to me. My parents had bought burial plots for both themselves and Callie years before at the cemetery behind First Baptist Church, which they'd attended their entire lives. My father, being my father and all that entailed, would want us to make a huge production out of their funerals, but I wasn't sure I had it in me to do that. I'd been forced to live through enough father-induced *big productions* in my life; I couldn't stand the thought of another one.

Smile, dammit! People are watching! People were always watching, from the sidelines of the annual county mud races, to the audience at the ribbon-cutting ceremony for the new civic center, to the people filling the pews of First Baptist Church. I'd ask Lena what she wanted, but I seriously doubted she cared, in which case I'd tell the funeral home no service of any kind. Just cremate them and get it over with.

The house, the land … it was all paid for, had been for years. I certainly didn't want it. I wondered if Lena would. Of course, if we ended up having to sell it to pay for an attorney, it wouldn't really matter what Lena wanted. We'd have to figure all that out, but there was time for that in the morning. What I wanted at that moment was a hot shower and a soft bed.

Back at the hotel, I'd locked the door behind me and headed for the bathroom, tossing my purse on a worn—but thankfully clean-looking—bed as I barreled my way through the tiny room. Setting the water as hot as it would go, I'd climbed in and stood under the spray for an eternity, trying to rid myself of the sights and scents of that morning, scrubbing until every bit of the sample-sized soap and shampoo were gone and my skin was red and steaming.

After toweling myself off, I'd dressed in my new undergarments and pulled back the covers with the intention of sleeping the rest of the day away, but as I'd moved to set my purse on the bedside table, the card, the one Bill Frazier had given Lena, had fallen out. I had told Lena I'd call the attorney, but surely that, too, could wait until morning.

I placed the card next to my purse and crawled between the covers, comforted by the cool, crisp sheets against my raw skin, then waited for the hum of the window unit to lull me to sleep. Instead, I heard Lena's voice. *Nowhere*, she'd said when I asked her where she was going. *And I can get there on my own.* Poor Lena had *always* been on her own; could I really do that to her now? We were all that was left; surely we could set aside our differences and support each other through the coming weeks.

Reluctantly, I'd tossed back the covers and dug my cellphone out of my purse, keying in the number. The man sounded as if he'd been asleep, but maybe that was my own subconscious yearning clouding my perception. After providing him a quick summary of Lena's situation, we scheduled an appointment for the coming Wednesday, and I'd made a quick entry into my calendar to remind myself to start looking for Lena sometime the following Tuesday. I knew from past experience she could be hard to find. That accomplished, I'd crawled back between the sheets and was just drifting off when the phone interrupted me again. I grabbed it without looking, thinking it was probably Brenda, returning my call and pissed as hell. I owed her an explanation, but I knew she'd understand.

"Rebecca?"

It definitely wasn't Brenda.

"This is Bill. Bill Frazier. They've gone to pick up Lena. I thought you'd want to know."

Chapter 9: Lena

I'D BARELY MADE it halfway to the bottoms when I heard the blip of a siren behind me. I wasn't surprised. Our men in blue didn't like hitchhikers, and although no one had stopped to help a lady in distress, I did have my thumb out, ever the optimist. I stopped, still facing forward, looking down the long, empty highway, refusing to look back. If they wanted to talk to me, they'd either have to pull up farther, or get out and walk to me. I waited, watching heat rise from the asphalt and feeling sweat drip down my cleavage. Then I heard the sound of tires crunching on gravel as the car moved forward.

"Lena."

It wasn't Bill, but I recognized the voice, nonetheless.

"You didn't say nothing, did you? About last Wednesday?" I hated the whine I could hear underneath his words.

"Relax, Lenny. I didn't say anything. But I will, if I need to."

The scrawny man alongside me blew out a breath, his long fingers gripping the wheel so hard the tips of his fingers were white. "That wouldn't be a good idea, Lena. Bad things can happen in jail. I'd hate to see something bad happen to you. Now come on; they're on their way." His Adam's apple bobbed as he spoke.

"What do you mean, they're on their way?"

"I mean they're coming to arrest you. Right now. Just heard it over the radio. They're on their way to the bottoms, will probably come right by here in the next four, five minutes."

"Shit, Lenny." I glanced around me, frantically looking for a place to hide, but there was nowhere. Cotton fields stretched away on either side; the long, straight rows offered no protection, the flowering plants just over a foot high. Besides, if they didn't get me today, they'd get me tomorrow. There was no point in running, and no place to run to, anyway.

"Quick, play like I'm arresting you," Lenny said, turning on his lights.

"Play like? How old are you, Lenny? Four? You mean how I play like you have a pee-pee?"

"Just do it," he hissed. "They're almost here." Keying the microphone, he straightened his shoulders and spoke in a deeper voice than the one I'd come to know. "Charlie one-oh-two to headquarters."

The radio crackled. "Go ahead, one-oh-two."

Lenny moved to exit the car, fooling with the handcuffs on his belt with one hand while holding the mic with his other. "I've got a ten-fifteen out on the highway. Requesting backup."

"Ten-four," the voice crackled back. "Units are on the way."

I wasn't sure exactly what they were saying, but I had a good idea and I didn't like the look on Lenny's face. Before I could make a move, he dropped the radio and slammed me face down over the hood of his cruiser, just as two more police cars topped the hill behind his cruiser with lights flashing and sirens blaring.

"Lenny, you're going to be sorry for this. I can guarantee you that." My lips stung, and I could taste blood.

"Keep your mouth shut," he said, breathing hard against my neck while he yanked my arms behind me and snapped on the cuffs. "Just go along with me, Lena, and you'll be fine. We both will."

"Is that right? Funny how I'm not feeling too 'fine' right now, Lenny." He was leaning against me so hard I could barely breathe, and I swear he was enjoying it. I highly doubted he pressed his crotch so forcefully into just *any* prisoner.

"I'll loosen them, but you have to act like they're tight, okay? I can help you if you'll let me. Trust me; it's better for me to do this than one of them."

"I have to admit I'm not feeling the trust, Lenny." I gasped, my lungs crushed against the hood. "Could be because you like to buy women from time to time. You're a dirty cop. You know it, and I know it."

"Our time together does just as much for you as it does me," he said, as he stood up straight to greet his coworkers. "You need money; I need sex. It works. It can keep on working, too, if you'll do what I say and keep your mouth shut."

"Are you even going to tell me why I'm under arrest? I'm willing to bet it isn't for prostitution."

"You know damn well why you're under arrest," he said. "Technically, until they prove you chopped the hell out of your family, you're being taken in on an outstanding warrant. But it's only a matter of time, Lena. Christ, why did you leave so much evidence behind?"

"What evidence? What the hell are you talking about?"

He ignored my question and began loudly rattling off my rights, all of which I'd heard before. He wasn't reciting them for my benefit, anyway, he was doing it for the three cops who'd come to assist with my arrest and were now surrounding the two of us.

The fight went out of me as he put a hand on my head and shoved me into the back seat. I'd known this was coming, of course, but I hadn't expected it quite so soon, and I wasn't sure how to feel about it. I'd been arrested too many times to remember, but never for something as horrible as this. I didn't know what to expect. I knew our police department well, and generally speaking, I trusted them. I always knew they were just doing their jobs, even when I didn't like it, and they always knew I was just trying to get by, even when my actions were illegal.

I even trusted Lenny, to some extent. Sure, he was a crooked cop, but he wasn't a violent crooked cop, at least not by the definition of *violent* I'd come to accept. He contributed financially to the various businesses operating down in the bottoms, and he paid well. Let's face it; he didn't have to. He could have forced me—could have forced any of us—to give him what he wanted, but he never had. He was afraid now because he knew he accounted for a part of the timeframe they were investigating. I couldn't blame him, but I didn't plan on ratting him out, not only because I was well aware bad things could happen in jail, but also because he was right; I benefitted from our arrangement as much as he did. I wouldn't tell anyone unless I had to.

A part of me refused to believe I'd actually be found guilty and sent to prison. I'd never physically attacked my parents, not even when I'd lived at home. God knows I'd wanted to, could almost feel the satisfying smack of my hand across my mother's face, fantasized about the *thud* a baseball bat across my father's head would make—it's true; I did—but I'd never done either of those things. I'd embarrassed them, humiliated them, accused them, stolen from them, and verbally assaulted them, but I'd never laid a hand on them, and I certainly wouldn't have murdered them. *Chopped*, Lenny had said.

Holy shit.

I wouldn't have. Would I?

The hours of their deaths were a blank to me. I hadn't felt anger towards my parents in years; they simply didn't exist in my world. I'd released all that about the billionth time they'd broken my heart. I don't even remember what had happened. I'd once said that to Dr. Lewis, that I didn't remember, expecting her to say something along the lines of, "Well, if you can't remember, it must not have been very important." But she didn't. Instead, she said, "Death by a million papercuts."

I'd heard the saying before, but never in that context. It was a perfect description. That's exactly how it was, and hearing her put it that way helped me define my childhood within my own head. My parents didn't beat us, although neither of them hesitated to use a belt, switch, or well-placed slap if they felt we deserved it. What ruined us—because Rebecca is as ruined as I am; she just shows it differently—was thousands, no, millions of tiny cuts. Harsh words, undeserved criticisms, deliberately hurtful observations, gleeful ridicule, a lifetime of neglect, an overdose of indifference.

I try to think of examples sometimes, to share with Dr. Lewis, but I can't. It's impossible to sit and dredge up something on command. The memories come at the most unexpected times, and are triggered by the most mundane of events. I'll see a mom take her daughter's hand to help the kid cross the street, and I'll remember neighbors bringing me home after finding me wandering down our winding country road. I was three, four at the most, and while I couldn't tell time, I knew I'd left home when the rooster woke me up, and was returned home by Mrs. Rose and Mr. Carter as the sun was going down.

I'd been gone all day, having simply wandered away, loving the feel of cool dew on my bare feet, crying when cool dew turned to sharp rocks and blackberry vines. I'd finally curled up in a ditch too exhausted to walk—too exhausted to *cry*—and that was when Mr. Carter had rumbled by in his old pick-up after a day in the fields and caught site of my pink nightgown among the cattails.

How can no one notice that? How can a family of five living in a home no bigger than twelve hundred square feet *not fucking know when their toddler is gone?*

I wasn't punished when I got home, nor was I hugged. I wasn't greeted at all. "Oh," my mother had said, standing from her position beside Callie, where she'd been suctioning out my sister's nose, part of Callie's nighttime routine. "Put her over there." She gestured toward the couch. "God, she's a filthy mess, isn't she? Lena, what in the world have you been doing all day to get so dirty? Don't mess up my couch. You go sit over there, instead." She pointed to the corner by the kitchen doorway and returned to her work.

Is that normal, I ask you? *Is it?* It was in *my* household.

What if, in a drug-fueled haze … what if subconscious desires were unlocked? What if old resentments bubbled to the surface?

No. I wouldn't have.

Would I? God help me, I just didn't know.

I might have. Goddamn it, I might have.

Thoughts swirled through my head in sync with the spinning lights.

Chapter 10: Rebecca

SOMETIMES I THINK my mother hated Callie as much as she loved her. Maybe she didn't love her at all; I think that's probably closer to the truth. I think Callie met some dark need my mother had. What that need was, I couldn't say. I was never close enough to my mother to ask such a question, and even if I had been, I don't think she would have known the answer. I *do* know my mother hid behind Callie. Callie was a built-in excuse for everything the rest of us had to deal with: my mother's bad temper, her lack of interest, her lack of affection. But love? No. If she'd loved Callie, she'd have wanted what was best for Callie. A lifetime spent sitting in a wheelchair watching cartoons couldn't have been best for Callie.

I used to think, when I was young, that had Callie not come along, my mother would have had more time for me. More *love* for me, because that's what I really wanted. Had Callie not been born, my mother could have read me stories and taught me nursery rhymes. She could have braided my hair and dressed me in pretty clothes, made sure my socks matched and my face was clean. She could have seen me not just as another drain on her time or energy, but as a daughter she could enjoy, maybe even love. But she didn't, and that was Callie's fault, or so I believed. Callie had ruined everything.

I know now that isn't completely true. No doubt Callie's birth threw my own life off course, but I don't think it's fair to blame her for my mother's lack of interest. As I've thought of it over the years, I've come to believe Callie offered my mother an escape into her true self. I'm not sure my mother really had it in her to give the sort of love I wanted, not to Callie, not to me, not even to my father. Certainly not to Lena, who was both unplanned and unwanted.

Callie's presence served to bring out the worst in my parents, but she can hardly be blamed for that. I'm convinced neither of them had a strong foundation to begin with. Maybe, if circumstances had been different, they would have stayed the course. Maybe they would have had the stamina to raise us, whether there were two of us or three, meeting enough parental responsibilities for us to come out of the experience on the better side of normal. We'll never know. That's the thing about shaky foundations: they're fine as long as there's no wind, but let a storm blow through and everything comes crashing down.

I responded to my mother's hostility by spending time with my father. He wasn't affectionate, but if I worked hard he was approving, which was nearly as good. There was a lot to do on our little farm, and I was a hard worker. I did everything my father asked of me, whether that was mowing, hoeing, picking corn, or cleaning the henhouse. I worked as hard as any son could have worked, and when he rewarded me with a gruff, "Much obliged for the help," I walked on air.

When I think of those days, I remember them as quiet. A *good* kind of quiet. We worked side-by-side and he appreciated me, and I appreciated that. It hurt me when he no longer wanted my help. Not only that, but I missed spending time with him. I missed *him*. When I was no longer allowed to work the farm with him, I was no longer able to see what I considered his authentic self. I was left with one of two personas: the unhappy family man, or the boisterous politician. I liked neither.

Even so, I didn't hate my parents. Certainly not the way Lena did. Were they perfect? Not by a long shot, but whose were? A coworker at the factory, young kid, once remarked that no one my age seemed to have good memories of childhood. He's probably right, but that was more because we were a product of the times than it was because we had bad parents.

That's just how things were done back then, in that part of the country. We weren't coddled. We were expected to earn our keep. It wasn't about children as individuals; it was about children as the property of the parents. Is that wrong? Well, in today's world it is, but it wasn't back then. And who's to say which way is right? We weren't spoiled, I can tell you that. Not like some kids I see these days. Sometimes, I think maybe it's a blessing I was never given the chance to have kids of my own.

No, I didn't hate my parents, even though their faults were evident. My issue, to the extent that I had one, was always Callie. Before you come running after me with pitchforks and burning torches, please try to understand. I can love my sister and resent my sister simultaneously. Surely, you can understand that. It's possible to hold two opposing views at the same time. Emotionally devastating—at least in my case—but possible.

Her life overtook mine. That's the bottom line, and I don't know how to say it any more clearly. Callie existed; therefore, I had to exist for her. *For her.* My whole *life*. That's a simple concept in the abstract, but not so much in reality. Think about it for a minute. Imagine that every decision in your life was made not for your benefit, but for the benefit of someone else at your expense. My life, whatever my life might have been without Callie, no longer existed. This was determined when I was only four years old.

Put that on your social media meme.

Maybe, just maybe, my life would have been shit regardless. I'm smart enough to realize that. Maybe my fantasies of a life in the suburbs with a husband and 2.5 children just weren't in the cards. Maybe I wasn't meant to sip cocktails on back decks with neighbors in an upscale part of town, while we gossiped and watched our kids play hide-and-seek in the evenings. Maybe I wasn't meant to make love in the soft light of a warm, autumn fire with the man I loved. Maybe I wasn't meant to gripe about a husband's dirty underwear left, for the hundredth time, in the middle of the bathroom floor.

Maybe not. Who knows? Still, I would have liked the chance to find out.

I was never given that chance.

Even so, that's better than Lena had it. In the eyes of my parents, I was keeper of the family, but Lena didn't exist at all.

All of this to say, when Bill called me to let me know what was happening, I vowed to do everything within my power to help my sister. She was all I had left, and I found myself feeling a tenderness for her, an *understanding* of her, I hadn't felt in many years.

"Rebecca? Are you there?" Bill sounded impatient. "I'm not supposed to be calling you, you know. I need to get off here before anyone walks in."

"I'm here," I answered. *Unfortunately*, I nearly added. "How did this happen so fast, Bill? How do you know it was her? You can't possibly have proof this quickly."

"She left goddamn bloody handprints everywhere," he said. "Proof doesn't get much better than that. But you're right. She's being arrested for an outstanding warrant. We'll be able to hold her on that long enough to run those prints."

"Why are you in such a hurry, Bill? Let the evidence come in and do things in the order they're supposed to be done."

"It's not that simple, Rebecca."

"Why not?"

He waited so long to answer I thought my phone may have dropped the call. "Has it crossed your mind, Rebecca, that you might be next?"

It hadn't. "Bill, you don't really think … ?

"I think we'd better not take the chance."

Oh, Lena.

Chapter 11: Brian Stone

I'D NO SOONER begun an online search for news of Ms. Rebecca Reynolds than my phone buzzed, the already-familiar number lighting up the screen. Assuming she'd thought of something else I might need to know, I answered briskly, "Yes?"

"She's been arrested," she said, her voice too loud, causing me to wince and hold the phone away. "Now what? I don't know what to do. They won't let me see her tonight—that's what Bill Frazier said—but what about tomorrow? Are you going to help us? Do you need a retainer? I really don't know how this works."

"Ms. Reynolds." I forced my voice to be low, calm. I'd had years of practice in dealing with hysterical family members. "Bill is right. Tonight she'll go through an intake process. It's just the usual stuff: an interview, fingerprinting, mugshot. They'll take her possessions and issue her a number and a jumpsuit."

I'd found relaying the process to worried family members often worked well to calm them. Without specifics to cling to, loved ones tend to envision jail as Dante's *Inferno* without the symbolism, a dark, terrifying place full of violence, lust, and greed. While Dante's identified sins do tend to lurk beneath the surface of prison populations, intake procedures at the rural county jail to which Ms. Reynolds' sister would be taken were a far cry from any of Dante's circles.

"I know this already," she said, her tone impatient. "This isn't the first time Lena has been arrested."

That surprised me. "Information such as this would have been helpful to know upfront," I responded, my own impatience evident.

"I would have told you during our appointment next Wednesday. You sounded harried earlier, as if I'd awakened you."

Sharp lady. Bonus points for use of the word "harried." I hadn't heard that one in a while.

"What I want to know," she said, "is when I can see her. I live four hours away, but I'm in a hotel tonight about an hour away. Can I see her tomorrow? Or should I go home? I can't afford to stay in a hotel for days on end."

"She's been arrested before, yet you've never visited her in jail?" It wasn't relevant to the case, but I was curious.

"No. We haven't been close. She's been arrested for things like propositioning undercover cops or writing bad checks. Half the time, I didn't even know about it until she was already out. The other half, I was too frustrated with her to have any desire to visit. But this is obviously different."

My curiosity temporarily satisfied, I answered her questions. "During her intake she'll be asked the names and birthdates of anyone she wants to have visit. If you aren't on the list, you won't be allowed to visit. There's also an application you'll need to fill out. We can get it Monday when she goes before the magistrate. Assuming her list includes you, you'll need to have photo identification when you visit. In short, go home until Monday. You won't be able to see her before then."

"You said 'we,'" she said. "'We can get it Monday.' So you *are* going to help us?"

"I am. I'll call you as soon as I find out the time, and if you're free, we'll talk either before or after." To my surprise, I found myself warming up, my brain clicking away, filing and sorting and prioritizing the way it had always done before … well, before I'd started to loathe my job.

"What about your retainer?" she asked. "Neither of us has money. We'll have the house, *their* house, and the farm, which we can eventually sell, but Lena has absolutely nothing in the way of savings, and I don't have much, either."

It was true I needed money; I'd been living off my own savings for the past few months. My tastes had historically been ridiculously luxurious, an ineffectual attempt to overcome my inferior pedigree. I suppose I'd thought if I chose a home in the right zip code, it would somehow cancel out the fact that I'd grown up in the wrong one.

Phillip and Anna, who had known me better than anyone, always teased me about my playboy lifestyle, calling me their own *puer aeternus*, eternal boy. I'd happily participated in the joke. But Phillip had killed Anna, and everything had changed. The setup was gone now, leaving only the punchline.

I needed to downsize, particularly given my ambiguity concerning my career. I simply no longer had the funds to support the lifestyle. More importantly, I no longer had the desire to live it. I glanced around my bedroom, taking it all in. Bohemian, the designer had said, and although it was outrageously expensive, I had liked it immediately. Bold colors, beautiful woodgrains. Nomadic. Tribal. Two descriptors I'd fully embraced, because I saw myself as nomadic, but tribal made me feel as if I belonged, as if I *connected.*

What I hadn't realized at the time was that it wasn't furniture that made me feel connected; it was my relationship with Phillip and Anna. It was sharing my life with them, entertaining them, bringing them into a world they otherwise would not have experienced. But they did the same for me. I was a nomad, but I could travel safely knowing an invisible tether—one made of love—kept me connected to the two of them and the tiny family they created. *We* created. Without them, I didn't give a damn about furniture, or zip codes, or much of anything else. Now my outrageously expensive, Bohemian-styled, nomadic, tribal furniture only caused me pain.

I needed to sell the condo, find another office, downsize all the way around. I'd known that for months, but had been too numb to act on it. Hell, who knew? Maybe a house on a farm was what I needed. For a brief moment I felt reckless, giddy, as if I'd broken free of the self I no longer recognized just long enough to catch a glimpse of someone else, someone I might like to know. The euphoria passed as quickly as it had arrived, but left enough adrenaline behind to get me through the next few days.

I quoted her a rate and a retainer—one significantly below my usual, but which I thought was fair, and more importantly, one I thought she could possibly afford—and she agreed. "I'll draw up a contract this weekend," I said, "and we'll talk more on Monday."

"Thank you, Mr. Stone," she said. "I'll wait for your call."

"Speaking of calls," I said, "Lena will be allowed to make one, so be prepared for that. You can let her know we'll be there Monday."

"She may make a call, Mr. Stone, but it won't be to me. Lena has no idea what my number is."

"This case just gets more and more interesting," I said. "I suppose you'll fill me in when we meet?"

"I suppose I'll have to, if we want to save Lena." She paused. "Save is probably the wrong word. I imagine it's too late for that. Good night, Mr. Stone."

I sat again at my computer, but this time I didn't search for Rebecca Reynolds. This time, for the first time in months, I logged into my bank accounts. I had some planning to do, maybe not that night, that week, or that month. But sometime in the future, I needed to make some changes.

Chapter 12: Lena

IT'S NOT BAD, our county jail. In fact it's actually kind of nice. Hell, I know just about all the staff, and a fair portion of the inmates, too. In some ways, it's like a family reunion. Except that we know each other better, and like each other more. How sad is that? But it's true. Three of the officers came by to say hello. Another offered me an extra blanket. No one in my family would have done that. No one would even have noticed I was shivering.

I'd never before been arrested for murder, given my one attempt at the age of seventeen was, unfortunately, unsuccessful. If anyone deserved to be murdered, that nasty son of a bitch did. Still, even though I'd never experienced it, I'd known enough people who had to be familiar with the routine. I'd go before the magistrate on Monday. After that, I assumed I'd have a preliminary hearing and be bound over. I wasn't sure how to feel about that. I wasn't afraid, if that's what you're wondering. After all, I had an ace up my sleeve.

I didn't want to give up Lenny, but if it looked like I needed to, I would. I wasn't sure exactly how the court process worked, but I was fairly certain paying to screw me and then arresting me within the same week wouldn't play well with the judge. If things got too heated, we'd have to find out.

So, I wasn't afraid. More than anything, I was curious.

I was allowed to make a phone call, but didn't. I'd given the attorney's card to Rebecca, so that wasn't an option—hell, they'd have taken it from me, anyway—and I didn't know Rebecca's number. I'd never had reason to know it, having never had a phone of my own. There was no cell service down in the bottoms, and even if there had been, I had no steady income with which to pay for a phone.

Would Rebecca be at the arraignment? Would she call the attorney? I honestly didn't know. Sometimes Rebecca was there for me; other times, she wasn't. I don't blame her entirely for that. I'm a handful, even in the best of times. But I know Rebecca resents me, resents feeling as if she's in some way responsible for me. I don't know how much of that has to do with my fuck-ups as an adult, and how much has to do with our childhood.

Rebecca *was* responsible for me back then, as much as anyone was. That was partly because I was one of her assigned chores, and partly because no one else ever gave a damn. She was the one who got me up in the morning, made sure I had breakfast. Made sure I was on the school bus. She helped me with my homework, and gave me lunch money. She wasn't always cheerful; sometimes, she was downright mean. But she was my lifeline. And then she left. As soon as

Rebecca finished high school, she moved out. I was twelve years old.

"You can stay here, but you'll have to pay rent," I remember my father saying, and Rebecca laughed.

"Pay rent to live here and raise your children? I don't think so."

"You have a responsibility to the family," my father said.

"It's not my problem you and Mom don't know how to use birth control. You'd think after Callie, you'd have learned. It's pretty clear neither of you is happy with your last birth control fuck up," Rebecca countered, surprising me not only with her response, but also with the language and vehemence with which she spoke it. My father was surprised, too. I knew this because on a typical day had one of us spoken that word, he'd have knocked us silly. By the time he'd collected himself enough to slap Rebecca she was gone, leaving me with the sting of her last words.

I won't lie; it hurt. Rebecca and I were never warm and fuzzy, but until then I hadn't realized I existed due to the poor planning of a couple who'd run out of condoms. For whatever crazy reason, I had actually thought I was a considered part of the family. I had no *reason* to think that, but I'd never really pondered my existence at all. We were a family; I was a kid in that family. Rebecca's words drove home the fact I was a kid who wasn't supposed to have been.

I didn't realize back then how much courage it must have taken for Rebecca to stand up to our father—I was too caught up in her revelation, and too worried about losing her—but I realize it now. None of us had ever defied my father up until that point. I don't think it had ever occurred to us that we could.

No one defied my father, not the police, the town council, or even the various and sundry committees blustering their way through First Baptist Church. But here she was, still just a kid, going against my father's wishes. Of course, so was I when I left home, and as it turned out, my rebellion rendered hers negligible, but mine might not have ever taken place without hers. Once she cracked open the door, I came barreling through.

Rebecca, always the responsible one, got a job in a factory the next town over and rented a low-income apartment that took half her paycheck. For the next couple of years I saw her every other weekend or so, whenever she stopped by to pick me up and take me to her place for the weekend. I loved those times. She was always broke; we ate peanut butter and crackers and watched her little black and white television set, fiddling with the rabbit ears every few minutes to try to get a decent picture. We camped on the living room floor because she had so little furniture. I enjoyed every minute of it and she seemed to, as well, in spite of the hurtful words she'd spoken about me to our father.

I dreaded Sunday evenings, when she took me home. It was like walking from warm sunlight into cold shadows. Rebecca's apartment, though small and unadorned, was bright and airy, the blinds rolled up and windows more often than not thrown open. Nothing was hidden. There were no cloaked insinuations or sharp-cornered words to avoid. We always sidestepped the topic of Callie and my parents—what was there to say?—but aside from that, spoke on any number of topics: favorite T.V. shows, the hottest bands, the meanest teacher at Hemmings Elementary

School (Mrs. Hatcher, we both agreed, a woman Rebecca said was a bitch even when Rebecca had been in school).

Home, on the other hand, was dark and dreary, with an undercurrent of discontent that was palpable. I found myself tripping over layers of unspoken accusations, drowning under the weight of my parents' unhappiness. I felt, always, as if my appearance induced within them a profound exhaustion. When they greeted me, if they greeted me, I heard the echo of resigned sighs beneath their words.

It would be easy to discredit me, call me paranoid, and no doubt Rebecca's words influenced my thinking. But how else to explain their utter disregard? Callie was time-consuming; that can't be disputed. She needed constant monitoring. She could choke to death on her own spit or suffocate if her head fell too far forward or have a stroke from a rogue blood clot if we failed to move her around enough. These things had been drilled into me.

I knew the innumerable ways we could lose Callie just as well as I knew the sky was blue, but what about the ways they could lose *me*? I could wander out of the house at the age of four. I could fall into the old pond behind the barn at the age of seven. I could be beaten and raped by the owner of Jim's Pub at the age of seventeen. There were ways to lose me, too, but no one seemed to realize that.

When I was fourteen, Rebecca's factory job vanished when the plant closed down. She was given the option to transfer to another facility about four hours away, and she jumped at the chance. I was brokenhearted, but I understood. That job paid good money back then, nearly $8.00 per hour. There was nothing else like that in our town, especially for someone with no degree or advanced training. I helped her pack up her little apartment, and she kissed me on top of the head—the one and only time she ever kissed me—and told me she'd be back, that we might not see each other as often, but she'd be back to visit, and I could still spend some weekends with her, maybe even the whole summer.

I didn't see her again for two years and only then because my father was hospitalized with the first in a string of heart attacks. I was down in the bottoms, smoking a cigarette and jockeying for room around a trash-barrel fire, when Rebecca drove up in her bright red Yugo, pulling off on the graveled shoulder before slamming the door and slipping and sliding down the bank to face me.

My first impulse was to jump up and hug her. I'd missed her terribly, those peaceful weekends at her apartment cemented in my memory as the best times of my young life. But as I stood and stepped toward her, the impulse quickly faded. The Rebecca facing me was the Rebecca who'd resented me, the one who used to yank too hard as she put my hair in a ponytail, the one who scrubbed my face too roughly before dragging me to the bus stop on cold school mornings, the one who impatiently shoved me away when I reached out in the dark of night, seeking comfort after a nightmare.

I think Rebecca might have loved me during those weekends at her place. They were voluntary, after all. She invited me because she wanted to. No one was nagging her to look after me. No one was yelling at her because my homework wasn't done or grounding her because she'd lost track of me. But as she barreled toward me across the rocky bank, her nails digging in when she grabbed my arm and yanked me to my feet, I could see that I was once again a burden. She'd been summoned home, tasked with finding me, the irresponsible one who didn't even know about my father's hospitalization. She was expected to take care of things—of me, of Callie—until our father was well enough to come home.

As I sat in jail that first long night, it occurred to me that maybe those weekend escapes to Rebecca's apartment hadn't been voluntary at all. Maybe she'd just been living up to her *family responsibilities*, as my father called it.

Once the thought crossed my mind, I couldn't get rid of it.

But I missed her, still.

Chapter 13: Rebecca

LET ME TELL you a story. Settle in, get comfortable. Pour yourself a drink and listen up.

Once upon a time, there was a young woman named Rebecca. She wasn't the fairest in the land, but she wasn't half bad. She had long dark hair, and wide-set blue eyes, and although she'd been teased for being skinny throughout her childhood, she'd come to appreciate the long lankiness of her legs. This was especially true at the close of a work week, when she'd don a pair of little white shorts and walk the four blocks to her local grocery to pick up a six-pack of Budweiser. Without fail, she was met by whistles and cat calls, sometimes from groups of farm-filthy men riding in truck beds, sometimes from the open door of the bar she'd always planned to visit, but had thus far lacked the courage to enter.

She was enough of a feminist to know she should feel offended.

But she didn't.

She felt young and free and pretty—and just sexy enough to put a little extra sway in her step.

For the first time in her life Rebecca had friends, lots of them, and none of them cared a whit about her family. It didn't matter that her father was the mayor or that her sister shat in her pants. No one cared. They only cared about Rebecca.

There was Brenda, who packaged the 1/8 inch solder joint copper fittings across the way from Rebecca; and Al, who drove the forklift and always helped Rebecca load the pallets. There was Gunheild, who came from somewhere overseas and was married to a man who'd at one time been stationed in Millington. Gunheild was an inventory coordinator, and while many people thought she was a bitch, Rebecca knew she was just passionate about her work. Sometimes Rodney joined them at the break table, his arms covered in copper dust. Others came and went. Turnover was high. The work was hard. The schedules were brutal.

And then one night, as Rebecca and Brenda and Gunheild and Rodney lit up for a quick smoke before the buzzer sounded, signifying the end of break, Adonis walked in. He was beautiful, tall and strong and blonde, with just enough scruffiness about him to keep him from crossing the line into too pretty.

As it turned out, his name wasn't Adonis. It was Francis, but only one person had ever tried calling him that, on the playground in Francis' kindergarten year. That boy, with the ironic name of Stacey, had earned enough from the tooth fairy that night to start a small college fund.

The occupants of Break Room Table #3 called him Frank.

Well, except for Rebecca. She called him the love of her life.

And he was. Lovely, that is.

The relationship developed quickly, and they embarked on not just a physical affair, but a mental, emotional, intellectual affair. They were soulmates, something Rebecca hadn't really believed existed until Frank rode into town in a red and white Ford F-150 and swept her off her feet amid the roaring noise and noxious dust of Miller Copper, Inc.

He was her perfect match. He was a part-time student at the local community college, working his way through a business degree. In the middle of Baptist Republican country, he was a Methodist and a Democrat, unapologetically liberal in his beliefs. He urged her to go back to school, assured her she could do it, told her she was smart and beautiful and funny and special.

She really began to believe him.

Her father would have hated him, had they ever met, but Rebecca had no intention of ever letting that happen. She didn't want to share him or her happiness, some superstitious instinct warning her that as soon as her family became involved, it would all be over.

But they had a way of butting in, anyway.

One frigid November morning, nearly two years into the relationship, Rebecca got a call from her mother. Her father had suffered a heart attack sometime the night before. He was stable, thank goodness, but had been admitted to the hospital for tests and observation. Her mother needed to be with him, but what to do with Callie? And, heaven help us, Lena?

Rebecca had spoken to Frank about Callie, of course. She'd even told him the day would eventually come when she was responsible for the care of Callie. After all, that was what she'd been told all her life, and besides, there was no one else to do it. Lena certainly couldn't. Lena hadn't yet gone full scale with her rebellion, but the signs were already there. Skipping school, smoking cigarettes, staying out all night.

Rebecca received weekly phone calls from her mother regarding Lena's transgressions, real or imagined, and while she clucked and sighed at the appropriate times, she wasn't sufficiently invested or involved to put much thought into her mother's gripes once she'd hung up the phone. Rebecca secretly believed her mother enjoyed complaining, and was convinced if it hadn't been about Lena, it would have been about something else.

She'd always known she'd eventually be responsible for Callie, but back then, she hadn't yet realized the extent to which she'd also be responsible for Lena. It hardly mattered. As she would come to learn, imprisonment is imprisonment; one doesn't become more imprisoned simply because the number of guards increases.

Frank had listened, appropriately concerned, and—as Rebecca's heart melted—had cupped her face with his hands and gazed at her with soulful blue eyes and assured her he'd stand beside her, come what may.

And he did, in the beginning. Of course she had to go see to her family. Of course he understood. He helped her pack. He hugged her close and kissed her goodbye. He said, "Call me if you need me. You know I'll be there." He even double- and triple-checked to make sure he had her parents' phone number and called her every night during the week to check in, to make sure she was okay, to tell her he loved her. He filled her in on gossip from the factory and made her laugh with his mocking impersonations. He listened and sympathized and agreed and reassured.

He did all of those things the first few times Rebecca was summoned home for this or that, some emergency or other. He did all of those things for nearly two more years, until he'd gotten down on one knee and proposed. Until she'd ordered invitations and flowers, and rented the community center and bought a dress.

And then, one night after a dinner during which he'd been uncharacteristically quiet, just as she was laying out napkin samples across the Formica countertop ("Do you think this is too pink? I mean, the roses on the cake will be pink, but this is *really* pink, more like *hot* pink ....") he said, "You know, I don't think I can do this."

She looked up, startled at first, misunderstanding. "It's all silly, isn't it? I mean who really cares about napkin colors?" She swept them into a pile, searching his face, the first thick, slimy tendrils of dread spreading through her chest and squeezing her heart as she realized he hadn't been talking about napkins.

"I'm sorry, Rebecca." He stared at the floor.

You bastard, she thought. You can't even look me in the eye.

"I do love you," he said, and she wondered what that meant, that word. Clearly, her definition of it had always been faulty. "I just don't think I can take on that sort of responsibility," he continued, as her stomach clinched, her intestines turning to water. "I didn't realize how much it was or what exactly it meant, until seeing you, all the time, having to run to take care of them. And that's only part time. Can you imagine what it'll be like when it's full time?"

I can, you dipshit. It'll be exactly like this moment, forever.

"We won't have a life," he said.

For a minute there, I actually believed I might.

"Your sister is a lifelong commitment," he said, "and you're so strong. God, Rebecca, you are. I respect and admire you so much for that, it's part of what I love about you, but I'm not sure I ..." He trailed off before coming to hold her close. She stood rigid, arms crossed over her chest, as he awkwardly pulled her against him. "I'm not that strong. I hate myself for it, but I'm just not. You understand, don't you?"

The really sad thing was, she *did* understand. Of course he couldn't do it. *She* couldn't do it, but she did, anyway. What choice did she have?

They didn't fight. She didn't even cry, certainly not that he ever saw. This time, *she* helped *him* pack. She flushed the stupid pink napkin samples down the toilet, cancelled invitation and dress orders, emptied her savings account paying penalty fees, and hid a thick envelope full of class catalogs and financial aid applications deep in the back of the linen closet, where—nearly three decades later, brittle and yellowed—it remained.

She never saw Adonis again; it was as if he'd disappeared overnight. For that, she was grateful.

There would be no bail. Lena was deemed a flight risk, which was certainly understandable. She'd remain in jail until the trial, which was tentatively set for early the following year. I returned to my apartment, resumed my work in the factory, had friends over for a beer or two at the end of each work week.

I plodded through the business of sorting through my parents' estate, sent thank you notes for the hundred or so sympathy cards I received, rented a boat and scattered my family's ashes deep in the middle of the Hatchie River.

What I did not do, was visit Lena.

Chapter 14: Brian Stone
Winter, 2016

I LOCKED THE door behind me and tossed my wallet and keys onto the kitchen table, shrugging out of my suitcoat and kicking off my shoes. I was exhausted. I'd had yet another fruitless meeting with Lena Reynolds. The trial was just over two months away, and thus far, I had virtually nothing to go on.

I yanked off my tie, unbuttoning my shirt and shedding it before stepping out of my slacks. I didn't even need to unbuckle the belt for that acrobatic feat. I'd lost a lot of weight in the months after Phillip's trial. I knew I looked like a walking cadaver, eyes hollowed out and skin pale. The stress of my current case certainly wasn't helping matters any. I made my way to the bar along one wall of my living area, reached underneath for a bottle, and poured myself two fingers of Lagavulin. Reconsidered, then splashed in two more. Extra calories, I told myself.

Here's what I knew:

Becky Reynolds had been decapitated with three quick, powerful blows.

Eugene Reynolds had multiple wounds, twenty, maybe as many as thirty. It was difficult to tell, they overlapped so much. Most were concentrated in the chest and stomach area, and most had occurred well after he was dead. He also had numerous defensive wounds, including three severed fingers on his right hand.

Callie Reynolds had been quite literally eviscerated before having her throat slashed.

I'll spare you the gory details.

Two of Lena's handprints, one from each hand, had been left in blood on the right side, interior wall beside the front door.

A bloody footprint, smeared and unidentifiable, was found on the front stoop. The prosecutor would say it belonged to Lena. I would hire an expert to argue the possibility that an unknown intruder had committed the crimes.

Upon arrest, five days after the murder, Lena had tested positive for Demerol.

Two items were confirmed missing from the property. The first was a small safe that, according to Rebecca, was missing from Mr. Reynolds' home office. "It held mainly personal family papers," she'd said. "Bank information, deeds, Callie's medical history, my parents' marriage certificate. That sort of thing."

"Money?" Bill Frazier had asked.

"Possibly," Rebecca confirmed, "but not much. Never over a thousand, usually much less."

The second item missing was an axe. Rebecca had initially balked at surveying the contents of the tool shed. She knew the reason she'd been asked to take inventory, and I knew it couldn't have been easy for her.

As it turned out, the axe was the only item she noticed missing, and that was only because she'd used it several weeks earlier to remove a tree root that made it difficult to wheel Callie to the family car. "It's an old cedar axe," she'd said. "Twenty-five inch handle, two pound head. I hung it back up right here." She'd pointed to a couple of nails high up on the wall. "I'm sure my father wouldn't have moved it. Since his last heart attack he hasn't been able to do the sort of work that would require an axe." She winced after she'd said it, and I wondered what dark thoughts were going through her mind.

I hadn't spoken to Rebecca much since the early days of the investigation, but I'd met with Lena numerous times since then. She was an interesting client, an interesting person in general. Smart, obviously, but resistant as hell. That would have been expected, had I been an attorney for the prosecution, but hell, I was trying to *help* her. I already knew, without a doubt, I didn't want to put her on the stand. I *needed* her on the stand, but she was too irreverent, too unrehearsed. It wasn't just that she lacked a social filter; it was that she reveled in shocking people, and I couldn't seem to make her understand her behavior would doom her in court.

The first time I met with her, she damn near threw herself on me. From rubbing her foot up my leg, to sucking on her finger, to caressing her own breasts, she seemed determined to get some sort of reaction out of me. Shock? Arousal? Who knew—I doubt even she knew. Whatever it was, I didn't oblige. I'd had a long and remarkable career; there wasn't much she could throw at me I hadn't previously fielded. By our fourth or fifth meeting she seemed to have given up on that front, but the successive one wasn't much better.

"You want me to say I didn't do it, but I can't," she'd said, "because maybe I did."

"What I want," I'd said, exasperated, "is for you to give me an alibi. Names would be even better. My job is to prove you couldn't have done it. A little help from you would be most appreciated. What I *don't* want is for you to tell me you might have done something I'm tasked with proving you didn't do."

"I already told you, I was with Willie G."

"When, exactly? Monday? Where were you Monday night?"

"All I can tell you is I woke up on the riverbank Tuesday morning."

"Was this Willie G. person there when you woke up?"

"No, but he had been."

"When did he leave?"

"I'd guess maybe a couple of hours before I woke up."

I sighed. "Lena, seriously."

"What?"

I stood, pacing the length of the room. "I can't build a defense based on your supposition that he *might* have been with you up until a couple of hours before you woke up. Before you woke up, Lena? Do you see the problem here?"

"He'd had sex with me," she said, raising her voice and sitting up straight. "Okay? When I woke up, it was pretty damn obvious he had recently had sex with me."

I turned to face her. God, what a fucked up life this woman had. I would have felt sorry for her if I'd had that luxury. As things stood, the best thing I could do for her was to set my pity aside and work on saving her life.

I lowered myself to my chair. "How do you know it was him?" I asked, striving for a more empathic tone.

She looked surprised. "Well, who else could it have been?"

I didn't answer right away, just sat and gave her time to let the implication sink in. She'd been passed out on a riverbank, completely vulnerable, exposed to any criminal element inclined to take advantage of such a situation, and God knew the bottoms were crawling with criminal elements. For all we knew, Willie G. could have been gone for hours by then. I didn't doubt that she'd been raped—interesting that she didn't use that word—but there was no way to prove Willie G. was the perpetrator, not without a rape kit in evidence, and not without Willie G., who we'd as yet been unable to locate.

"It was Willie G.," she said, her tone angry. "Why do you think he gave me drugs? It wasn't out of the goodness of his heart, I can tell you that. That's not how things work down in the bottoms. If you people would do your damn jobs and go find him, he'd tell you that, too."

Even if we could find him, I was fairly confident he wouldn't admit to raping a woman he'd drugged into unconsciousness. Still, he was all we had, or hoped to have, anyway. At that point, our entire case rested on Willie G. I, more than anyone, wanted him found.

Lena had no idea where he was from originally.

"Texas, maybe?"

She didn't know if he had any family in the area.

"Not that he ever talked about."

She didn't know where he lived.

"He's just there, you know? Hanging out in the bottoms like everyone else."

She didn't even know what the *G* stood for.

"I don't know. That's just what everyone calls him."

"Lena, you've got to give me something."

"He's not that hard to find," she said, her voice shrill. "He's pretty damn noticeable. Over six feet, can't weigh more than one thirty, one thirty-five. I've told you all this." She stopped and took a deep breath. "He always wears a Tennessee Volunteer's baseball cap," she said, her voice softer, sounding resigned. "Used to be white, but is so dirty it looks black. Has a bushy beard, reddish brown. Doesn't have any teeth. How can you miss all that? Shit, you could *smell* him from a mile away. Is anyone even *looking* for him?"

"They are, Lena, but you know how transient that crowd is. No one knows anything about anyone else. People come and go all the time, and it isn't as if anyone down there is eager to talk to the police. Is there anyone else you can think of, anyone who may know where he is?"

"I don't know," she said, rubbing her forehead as if it ached. "I'm tired, Brian. Can we do this some other time?" We'd ended it, then. I was tired, too, mostly of feeling as if out of the two of us, I was the only one who gave a damn about her case.

Picking up my glass I walked over to the couch and sat, leaning my head back, letting the warm comfort of good Scotch soothe me. We had two months until the trial, and I had so little to work with. The thing was, I believed she was innocent. Yeah, I know all defense attorneys believe their clients are innocent, but I truly did. I had a working theory I had to get in order, fill in some pieces. It was a crazy theory, but if I could orchestrate it properly, it would make sense. It had to; it was all I had.

She'd been at the crime scene. There was no disputing that. Handprints don't lie. But I didn't think she'd been there alone. I thought she'd been there with the killer.

We needed to find Willie G.

Chapter 15: Lena

I NEEDED TO see Dr. Lewis. She'd kept our regular appointment times, coming to the jail to conduct our sessions, but I couldn't wait until our next appointment. I needed to see her *now*.

I'd had a dream. No, not a dream, a fucking *nightmare*. I'd woken up screaming and hadn't stopped since. The guards didn't seem to know what to do with me, which wasn't surprising, since I didn't even know what to do with myself. I couldn't stop. It had been so real. I could still see it, feel it, *smell* it. I stopped screaming long enough to puke between the bars.

I don't know who finally decided to call Dr. Lewis, but when I was finally escorted to the visitor's section she was sitting there waiting for me, her hair smashed flat on one side, no make-up on her face. I'd have ordinarily razzed her about that, but this was no ordinary visit.

"Lena, what happened?" she asked, standing as the night guard led me in and stepped away. "I got an emergency call—"

"I saw them," I said, cutting her off.

"Sit down," she said, taking her own seat across the table. "Tell me who you saw."

"I saw ..." I tried to tell her, but the bile rose in my throat. "Callie," I managed to say, closing my eyes as if that could erase the image, when in reality it only highlighted it. "And my parents."

"When, Lena? Why are those images so troubling to you?"

"Because they were dead," I nearly screamed. "Dead. Bloody. Mutilated."

Dr. Lewis shook her head as the guard stepped forward, and he retreated. "You've had quite a shock," she said. "It's not unusual to have nightmares after such—"

"No!" I interrupted her. "I was there. I was there when they were killed."

"Lena." Her voice sounded cautious, careful. "We know your prints were there. Remember? You were there at some point, but that doesn't mean you did it."

I shook my head, so agitated I could barely speak. "I think I did it," I whispered. "I think I *did* it," I said, louder this time, bordering on a shriek.

"Why do you believe that?" Dr. Lewis leaned forward and reached across the table as if to take my hands in hers, but I snatched them away.

"My hands." I gagged, holding them up in their cuffs, shaking them as if they weren't a part of me, as if I needed to be rid of them. Sweat prickled my scalp, trickling down my forehead. "There was blood on my hands, blood *everywhere.* Oh, my God, it was *everywhere.*"

"What else did you see, Lena? Focus on me. What else did you see? This is important. I need you to concentrate."

But I couldn't. Dr. Lewis was floating away from me, spinning off into outer space. Vaguely, I was aware of her motioning for the guard. I remember fighting, being restrained.

I don't remember anything else.

Chapter 16: Rebecca

BACK IN THE spring, several months before my parents were killed, I found my father sitting in a lawn chair under an elm tree on the far southwest corner of the farm. I'd looked everywhere for him before an old memory surfaced, a memory so old I wasn't entirely sure if it was remembered, or dreamt.

In the memory, or dream, it was just the three of us, my mother, father, and me. I was skipping. I remember that clearly. I'd only just learned how, and I was taking great pleasure in performing huge, leaping strides over clumps of wild-growing daffodils and jonquils, enjoying the breeze and the sound of my parents laughing. We were headed toward the elm on the back of the farm. My mother carried a quilt, a faded yellow and blue star pattern held close in front of her growing belly, and my father carried an old, wooden picnic basket. It was one of those memories that seems too good to be true, but it was there, tucked into a back corner of my consciousness.

On the present spring evening, exhausted and irritable after a Saturday morning of doing yardwork for my father and an afternoon of running errands for my mother, I followed my instincts to the old elm. My father was there, sitting quietly, and I took a seat on the ground beside him. He was dressed in an untucked button-up shirt, an old pair of khaki pants, and loafers so worn out they'd gone from black to gray. He never had been good at casual wear, not even back in his farming days, preferring starched shirts to the worn coveralls and denim other farmers wore. I was sure that said something about him, pointed to some insecurity, but I'd never attempted to explore the issue with him.

He was always a taciturn man when not in front of a crowd, and that day he'd seemed especially reticent, curtly outlining my list of chores before leaving me alone with my work. He spared me a glance as I sat, maybe even a slight nod, but said nothing. I didn't speak, either, just sat cross-legged, enjoying the view of gently sloping fields, freshly plowed and waiting for soybeans. Something about our shared space reminded me of my childhood, back when I helped him plow and hoe and pick, before he'd banished me to the house to help my mother.

"Remember when you used to work with me out here?" he asked, as if reading my thoughts. "You were a big help. Hardworking. Did as much as any boy could have done, and probably stronger than half of them."

I was surprised at the compliment; that wasn't my father's style. "I remember," I said. "I enjoyed it. It was nice, working out here with you." It felt odd to be so candid with him, but it was true. It had been nice.

He grunted, but said nothing. I had a feeling he wanted to talk with me about something specific; he'd never made small talk with his children. I waited.

"Your mother is sick," he said. "Cancer. She let it get away from her. Had blood in her stool the last year, but never would make an appointment with the doctor. By the time I got her to go, it was too late."

Too late? "You mean ..."

"Three months, maybe. Maybe six. No way to know, is what the doctor said. She's not hurting. Not yet, anyway. Says she isn't. But it's just a matter of time."

"Daddy, I—"

"Nothing you can do to fix her," he said with a wave of his hand. "Just thought you should know. With my heart the way it is, I'm going to need some help. Can't take care of Callie and this place. Not by myself."

I'd known the time would come, of course, but it had always seemed far off, something I could put on a back shelf to worry about another day. Now that day was apparently here.

"Rebecca," he said, and cleared his throat. I looked at him, my eyebrows raised, waiting. "Was I a bad father?" he asked, and I picked up on something in his voice, a softness I'd never heard before. "I think I must have been," he said quietly, nodding, as if to himself. "I do believe I was." He pulled a handkerchief from his back pocket and wiped at his eyes.

My father could work a crowd into cheers and whistles when he had his political suit on, but at home, with us, he was stoic. Distant. I'd seen more vulnerability in my father the past five minutes than I had in my lifetime.

When my initial shock dissipated, I struggled with another dilemma. He'd asked a question, and some small, dark part of my heart wanted to answer it honestly. *Yes*, I wanted to say. *You were. You were cold and absent and disapproving. Instead of a real father, you were a façade, whatever the constituents wanted you to be. You made us smile when there was nothing to smile about, paraded us around as if we were your sideshow. We were fodder for voters, pretty faces on campaign posters, only to be dismissed and forgotten once the Rotary fundraiser was over, Miss Teen Soybean was crowned, the Busy Bees had pledged twenty quilts to the local Red Cross Shelter, and the show was a wrap, the cameras and microphones packed away. As soon as we stepped out of the spotlight, we ceased to have value. We weren't individuals; we were tools, used until no longer useful, then tossed aside, broken and neglected.*

I remembered Lena crying her first day of kindergarten. She had no backpack, no lunchbox, and no supplies, as if no one had remembered or even realized she'd be starting school. My mother was consumed with Callie, with suctioning out her nose, braiding her hair, checking and re-checking her pill box, filling out paperwork for her various medications, and writing pages of notes and instructions for her teachers.

Callie was going into second grade that year. At least that's what her records said, but she wasn't really. In reality, she was going into the same room of students she'd had for both her kindergarten and first grade years, a room full of students with varying disabilities and of varying ages, a room in which Callie would sit strapped in her chair in a corner out of the way, ignored until the odor of her soiled diaper re-minded someone she was there.

I'd given Lena my own notebook, college-ruled and inappropriate, leftover from the year before, along with a pencil much too thin for her fingers. I managed to find enough change in the cushions of the couch to pay for her lunch, if not for mine.

Another memory in the never-ending reel: my father changing the locks when Lena was sixteen years old. I was home for the weekend seeing to Callie. I'd been angry at my youngest sister's absence, jealous, to tell the truth. I lived four hours away and couldn't seem to escape my family, while Lena, who lived in the same damn house, somehow managed to escape just fine.

She'd become a public embarrassment by then, and that was the tipping point for my father. He made a big production of going to town, returning with a couple of deadbolt locks he screwed into place on the front and back doors. Later that night he stood watching her through the back door glass, downright gleeful at the moment she realized her key no longer worked.

Lena was belligerent, defiant, the tears long de-pleted. For a moment she looked as if she would smash her way in, but then she left, stalking down the long gravel drive on her way to who knew where.

I remembered my father's responses when I wanted to do what the other kids did. Work on the homecoming float. Go to the game. Go to prom. Go to college. *Who's going to help your mother?* Always the same question, to which I never had a satisfactory answer. *She has her hands full with Callie, and you have a responsibility to your family.* I strained against his philosophy back then, believing I could someday be free. But I came to accept it later. As much as I'd tried to run from it—from *them*— it—and they— always managed to catch me.

I remembered his angry slap when I was thirteen years old and squirmed away from Mr. Cooper, an impossibly ancient man whose gnarled, yellow fingers and foul breath made me recoil. *You won't embarrass me in public*, my father said. *Act like you have some manners, girl. Do you know who he is? That's the banker. Hell, he funded half my campaign.* I remembered the next time Mr. Cooper reached for me, how I looked at my father's warning eyes and acquiesced. I remembered Mr. Cooper's arms encircling my waist, pulling me onto his lap, the hardness against my bottom something I didn't comprehend until later.

I remembered my father forcing me to accept Mr. Cooper's Sunday invitation to lunch.

I remembered the next Sunday, when he invited Lena instead of me.

She was seven years old.

I wondered if, prostituting herself down on that riverbank, Lena also remembered.

I sat under the elm and listened to a bobwhite's lonely call from somewhere in the branches over my head. *Bob-white!* An answering call soon followed from a stand of cedars behind the toolshed. When I was young I used to mimic that call, thumb and middle finger stuck in my mouth, holding my tongue flat. Every so often it worked, and I'd spend part of an evening halfway up the pecan tree in our front yard, holding court with the quail, our traded whistles floating across the pasture.

I watched the shadows stretching down the furrowed rows in front of us, smelled the aromas of soil and freshly cut grass. Butterflies flitted around fallen apples underneath the old apple tree. A more idyllic scene could hardly be imagined.

I studied my father, who looked old and tired and worn out. "You were fine, Dad," I said. I opened my mouth to say more. Closed it. Watched a ladybug wobble her way up a dandelion stem at my feet. We used to make wishes on dandelions, Lena and I, closing our eyes to blow dried seeds across the grass. Sometimes I wished for a handsome prince to sweep me into his arms. Other times I wished for a puppy of my own—not a mangy, smelly farm dog, but a puppy with a bright red ribbon tied in a bow at the back of his neck. Most often, I wished for Callie to be normal. If only Callie could be normal, I thought, everything else would fall into place.

"You were fine," I said again, barely able to force the words from my throat. I bent forward to send the ladybug on her way with a puff of breath before digging the weed up with my fingers. Best to get rid of it while it was alive; otherwise, the seeds would spread and make more work for me.

I could have held my father accountable, leveling my accusations, but what was the point? As I've said before, it simply *is*. Things simply *are*. The past can't be undone. My parents were old, and they were dying. There was nothing to be gained by dredging up the past.

My father nodded, seemingly satisfied, and went back to staring across the fields while I ripped away at the roots.

Chapter 17: Brian Stone
May, 2016

"WE WILL SHOW you"—John McDonald pivoted toward the jury—"that Lena Reynolds not only had opportunity, she also had motive."

I sat next to Lena at the defense table and concentrated on my breathing. I didn't feel well; my stomach churned and my chest was tight. I wasn't worried about the prosecutor; he wasn't the cause of my distress. He was known as a distinguished and experienced attorney, true, but so was I. I'd been on opposite sides of the courtroom from him before, and my clients had both walked out as free men.

McDonald paced in front of the jury, outlining his case. I had to admit, on paper it sounded good. It sounded damn near impenetrable, if I'm honest about it. But I had my own hypothesis about what happened that night, and my beliefs didn't jive with his. If only we could find Willie G., or even find someone who knew his real name. Thus far our efforts had failed, and without him my defense would be much harder to mount. Harder, but not impossible.

John McDonald pivoted again, his signature move, I remembered, and his jacket flapped behind him. He could have easily fit the role of an absent-minded professor: ill-fitting suit, thinning hair, rumpled tie, crooked wire-rimmed glasses, all of which may have seemed inconsequential, but wouldn't be to the jury.

My own suit was exquisitely tailored; my shoes soft, buttery leather; my nails filed and buffed, my hair freshly cut with just enough silver curls in evidence to render me charming to the jury. I may have been struggling on the inside, but on the outside, I was copacetic. More than copacetic, I was handsome—boyish enough to appeal to older women, sexy enough to attract the younger ones, masculine and athletic enough to command respect from men of all ages.

Ostentatious? Absolutely, but also meticulously calculated. As I used to tell Anna when she teased me, I'm not as shallow as I appear. Studies—which I make a point of studying—indicate that attractive, prosperous-appearing professionals are more successful, and I dress to succeed. Every advantage counts, no matter how insignificant it may seem. This is true in all walks of life, but particularly worth noting when a client's life hangs in the balance. I'd always taken my responsibilities very seriously, and because of that, I'd won a hell of a lot of cases. We'd win this one, too. I'd save Lena even if it killed me, which I thought it very well might.

When I'd first agreed to take on the case I'd assumed the trial would be held in Lena's hometown, in the majestic old courthouse on the town square of the county seat. But given the population of the town, coupled with the massive media coverage, it just wasn't possible. Lena's family had roots in that town. They were a well-known, well-connected family. Hell, her father spent over two decades as sheriff and eight years after that as the town's mayor. Her mother had served for years on the town's botanical committee. As I learned during my research, several years before Lena was born Becky Reynolds had literally planted the dogwoods and redbuds that still adorned the courthouse's sprawling front lawn. I'd had no choice but to file a motion to request a change of venue.

Media coverage was still intense, and calls of "murderer" and "sinner" had rung out from the crowd on the sidewalk as we'd made our way into the building. One enterprising graffiti artist had spray-painted the fifth of the Old Testament's Ten Commandments on the sidewalk, *Honor your father* clearly visible in the bright morning haze as city workers labored to scrub away the paint before pedestrians tracked red footprints down the city sidewalk. Even with all that, the request had worked out well for Lena, certainly better than she would have faced had we stayed in her hometown.

Not so much for me, however.

Upon learning of the change of venue, the assigned courtroom, the presiding judge, I'd very nearly dropped the case, although that wasn't something my client knew. Instead of a stately, southern, red-brick courthouse, we'd be in the more modern steel and brick compound in which I'd spent the majority of my career. The prospect of re-entering that building had left my knees weak and my palms damp.

I couldn't imagine stepping through those heavy doors and hearing the quiet *swoosh* as they closed behind me, a sound that used to excite me but now filled me with dread. I couldn't fathom sitting at that oak table with its lemon-scented polish, looking at the leather seat next to me and instead of Lena, seeing the ghost of Phil. I'd failed Phillip in that courtroom, not because I'd lost the case—we'd have won it; of that, I'm sure—but because I couldn't save him from himself.

Fidelity, I'd whispered.

Fealty, he'd answered in return.

And I'd meant it, even if it meant losing him.

There are ten divisions of criminal court in our criminal justice complex, and over the years I've spent time in all of them. But I hadn't set foot in the ninth division in over two years, having either transferred cases that could have taken me there, or negotiated plea deals that kept me elsewhere. I'd done my best to avoid the entire floor, my breath constricted even as the number lit up on an elevator I happened to occupy.

I don't know why I didn't drop the case upon receiving information regarding the venue, other than my previously mentioned sense of responsibility. I'd made a commitment; I'd see it through. I'd known, of course, there was a chance—a decent chance—I'd end up in Judge Wallace T. Fuller's courtroom, but I'd hoped the gods would be kind. If anyone should have known the folly of holding such hope, it should have been I.

"You've lost weight," Rebecca had said to me outside the courtroom doors. We'd spoken by phone a few times, but hadn't seen each other in months.

"Are you ill? I only ask because I need to make sure you'll be here in the long-term for Lena. I don't mean to pry." She, by contrast, looked lovely, like a sophisticated, polished version of her sister, dressed in an ivory suit and pearls with the slightest hint of sadness evident just around her eyes. I wondered again what quirk of nature caused these sisters to grow up two sides of the same coin, one responsible to the point of self-sacrifice, the other irresponsible to the point of self-destruction.

I managed a smile. "I always drop a few pounds before trial," I reassured her. "I'm running on adrenaline. Ready to get this party started?"

"No," she'd answered, "but I don't seem to have a choice."

I sat, listening to the prosecutor make his opening statement and jotting notes on the legal pad in front of me in order to methodically deconstruct the theories put forth by the state, all while feeling sweat dampen my armpits. Beside me, Lena was dressed in an olive-colored pencil skirt and cream-colored blouse, an outfit donated by her sister and totally out of character for her. She sat with her hands clasped in her lap and one leg crossed over the other, swinging her foot hard enough and high enough to stir the air and occasionally bang against the table. I put a hand on her arm, glanced toward her foot, and gave a nearly imperceptible shake of my head. I could tell by her expression she didn't care for my subtle reprimand, but for the moment, her foot stilled.

If my discomfort was internally contained, Lena's was anything but. She jittered and fidgeted and turned in her chair, craning her neck as she looked out over the assembled crowd. She picked at her cuticles and fumbled with the buttons on her blouse, alternately sighing and yawning. I needed her to remain still, to portray the perfect balance of grieving daughter, law-abiding citizen, and concerned seeker of truth. What I really needed—though I knew better than to suggest it—was for her to behave like Rebecca.

"We have a witness," John McDonald was saying, "who will testify that she saw the defendant walking west down Bucktail Road toward the river bottom and away from town at approximately three o'clock on the morning of Tuesday, July fourteenth, two thousand fifteen. The witness will testify that she saw blood on the hands and arms of the defendant at that time. The medical examiner will testify that the Reynolds family was murdered between July thirteenth and July fourteenth of that same year …"

I settled in, my heartrate beginning to slow, my stomach settling. It was game time, the formality of the courtroom calming, the age-old process familiar and comforting. I could almost feel Phillip beside me, sitting composed and resigned in Lena's leather chair. *You can do this*, he'd say, his tone earnest, his expression intense, convincing me of my own abilities, my own *worth*, just as he always had.

You got this, ghost-Phillip said to me before disappearing, leaving only Lena staring back at me.

I stood and faced the jury as the prosecutor took his seat.

Phillip had never lied to me, and I didn't think ghost-Phillip would, either. I trusted him beyond this realm and into the other, just as he had trusted me.

I got this.

Chapter 18: Trial Transcript

Court Clerk: Can you state your name for the record, please?

Sandra Peavy: Sandra Jean Peavy.

Court Clerk: Spell your last name for the record, please.

Sandra Peavy: S-A-N-D-R-A.

Court Clerk: Your last name, Ma'am.

Sandra Peavy: Oh, I'm sorry! [laughs] I'm just so nervous. It's P-E-A-V-Y.

Court Clerk: Thank you.

The Court: Just relax, Ms. Peavy. Everything will be fine. Your witness, Mr. McDonald.

Prosecutor: Thank you, Your Honor. Good morning, Ms. Peavy.

Sandra Peavy: Good morning.

Prosecutor: Do you know the defendant, sitting over there?

Sandra Peavy: Yes, sir. Kind of. I mean, we're not like best friends, or anything, but I see her around. We hang out in the same group, is what I mean. Lena Reynolds, but we call her Hootchie.

Prosecutor: How long have you known Ms. Reynolds?

Sandra Peavy: Oh, forever. Years. Since she first showed up down in the river bottoms years and years ago.

Prosecutor: You stated "we call her Hootchie." Who, exactly, calls her Hootchie?

Sandra Peavy: Everyone. All of us.

Prosecutor: You mean everyone who makes their residence down in the river bottoms?

Sandra Peavy: If you mean everyone who lives down there with us, then yes.

Prosecutor: Why does everyone call Ms. Reynolds Hootchie?

Defense Attorney: Objection. Calls for speculation. Ms. Peavy can't possibly know the motivation of everyone else living in the river bottoms.

The Court: Sustained. Rephrase, Mr. McDonald.

Prosecutor: Ms. Peavy, why do you call Ms. Reynolds Hootchie?

Sandra Peavy: Because she's … I don't know if I'm allowed to say this. Can I say it?

The Court: Go ahead, Ms. Peavy.

Sandra Peavy: Okay. Well, it's because she's sort of a slut. A prostitute. I mean, we all do what we have to do, so I'm not judging her. No, sir. But she sleeps with people. Has sex with them, I mean. Men. So they'll give her drugs.

Prosecutor: Have you seen Ms. Reynolds take drugs?

Sandra Peavy: She takes drugs all the time. Tokes up, shoots up, whatever.

Prosecutor: Have you ever seen Ms. Reynolds become violent when she's under the influence of drugs?

Sandra Peavy: Word on the street is she tried to kill a man back when she was a kid. I didn't see it personally, though.

Defense Attorney: Objection. Complete hearsay. More prejudicial than probative, and totally irrelevant to this case. Move to strike from the record. Your Honor—

The Court: I hear you, Mr. Stone. Sit down and calm down before I find you in contempt. The objection is sustained. The witness's last statement will be stricken from the record. To the members of the jury: disregard that last statement. You may continue, Mr. McDonald, but do so carefully.

Prosecutor: Thank you, Your Honor. I have no further questions.

The Court: Mr. Stone, your witness.

Defense Attorney: Good morning, Ms. Peavy.

Sandra Peavy: Good morning.

Defense Attorney: You've testified that Ms. Reynolds trades sex for drugs. Is that correct?

Sandra Peavy: That's what I said.

Defense Attorney: Have you ever seen Ms. Reynolds trade sex for drugs?

Sandra Peavy: You mean like actually watch her do it?

Defense Attorney: That's what I mean.

Sandra Peavy: God, no. Why would I want to see that?

Defense Attorney: Have you ever seen Ms. Reynolds have sex?

Sandra Peavy: No! That's disgusting.

Defense Attorney: Have you ever seen Ms. Reynolds do drugs?

Sandra Peavy: I haven't sat there and watched her shoot up, if that's what you mean.

Defense Attorney: Have you seen her snort drugs?

Sandra Peavy: No.

Defense Attorney: Have you seen her smoke drugs? Crack, for instance?

Sandra Peavy: No, but I don't have to see it to know she's doing it. Hell, she's high as a kite half—

Defense Attorney: Just answer the questions, please. You're testifying that you've never personally seen Ms. Reynolds trade sex for drugs. You're also testifying that you've never watched Ms. Reynolds have sex, nor have you watched her—

Prosecutor: Objection. Counsel is badgering the witness.

The Court: Sustained. Move along, Mr. Stone.

Defense Attorney: Is it fair to say you haven't person-ally seen Ms. Reynolds do any of the things you've accused her of doing?

Prosecutor: Objection.

The Court: Overruled. I'll allow the question.

Sandra Peavy: I haven't seen her personally, as you say, but—

Defense Attorney: Thank you, Ms. Peavy. I have no further questions, Your Honor.

Chapter 19: Rebecca

THE FIRST FEW days of court proved to be even more awful than I'd feared. I'd known my sister was no angel, obviously, but having a parade of people confirm it was difficult to sit through. I heard her described as a druggie, a slut, a weirdo, and a criminal. As the prosecutor tried to paint a picture of my sister's intense hatred for my family, I learned some of the awful things she'd said not only about my parents, but about me.

"You can't take it personally, Rebecca," Brian said during one of several phone calls.

"How else should I take it?" I asked. "According to that one witness, the one with what looked like a bad case of mange, Lena described me as an 'uptight bitch.' That sounds pretty personal to me."

"They're going to look under every rock, examine every nook and cranny, to find anything they can to make Lena sound like a drugged-out murderer. It doesn't matter if she said it twenty years ago or last week. It doesn't matter if she was angry, hungry, scared—whatever—when she said it. I'm willing to bet there are times over the years you've said a thing or two, maybe called her a name or two, in anger."

He had me there. "I know," I said. "You're right. This is just so hard. I want it to all be over."

"As hard as this is," Brian said, "what comes next will probably be harder."

"Why do you say that?"

"Because right now he's just building his case," said Brian. "Laying the groundwork, as it were; setting the stage. Some prosecutors start with the crime, shocking the jury with autopsy photos first thing to grab their attention. That's not how McDonald works. He's a storyteller. He'll lead the jury through getting to know Lena—the drug-addled, violent, family-hating Lena he wants to present. Once he has the jury convinced she has the temperament of a cold-blooded murderer, he'll show them what he believes to be her handiwork."

"Crime scene photos?"

"And autopsy reports. He'll call in his expert witnesses. Police who worked the crime scene will describe what they experienced. The medical examiner will give detailed information about each and every wound to your parents and sister. He's already convinced the jury Lena is a bad person; now he'll show them just how bad she is."

My stomach flipped at the thought. "How do we fight this? What do we do?"

"We find the real murderer before it gets to that point."

Chapter 20: Lena

MY CELLMATE SNORED and muttered in her sleep, but that wasn't what kept me awake. Patty Sue kept me awake. Patty Sue Wells, as I'd learned that afternoon when she took the stand to testify against me. Funny, I'd never considered her last name. She'd just been Patty Sue with the ratty hair and fried apple pies, Patty Sue who hoped to save our souls for The Good Lord. Patty Sue who now seemed bent on sending mine to hell. Her testimony played over and over in my head.

Did you see the defendant walking down Bucktail Road on the morning of July 14, 2015?

I did.

What time was that, Mrs. Wells?

It was 3 o'clock in the morning. I know exactly what time it was, because I'd gotten a call from my daughter. She'd gone into labor and I was on the way to the hospital to meet her.

Congratulations on your grandchild, Mrs. Wells.

Thank you.

Now, was anyone with the defendant when you saw her?

No. She was alone.

Did you notice anything on her hands and arms?

I did.

What was that, Mrs. Wells?

Blood. She had blood smeared all over herself.

When Brian had told me before the trial that a witness had seen me walking toward the bottoms with blood on my arms, I don't know what, exactly, I'd thought. I suppose I'd thought it was impossible, because I had no memory of it. But here was Patty Sue telling everyone I'd spent the witching hour doing a zombie impression, shuffling and stumbling aimlessly along the side of the dark road. Brian felt good about his cross-examination, but it didn't do much to get Patty Sue out of my head.

Did you speak to her?

No, sir, I did not. I didn't know what she'd gotten herself into, but I knew it wasn't safe to stop in the middle of a pitch black road down in the bottoms to ask. I planned to call the police when I got to town, but then with the baby coming and everything happening so fast, I plumb forgot.

Did you stop the car at all?

No, sir.

How fast were you driving?

The speed limit down there is forty-five, so that's what I was driving.

Driving at forty-five miles per hour on a dark road, you were able to not only identify the defendant, but also to deduce she had blood on her hands and arms?

I'd heard Rebecca shift in her seat at that point, from her place in the row behind me. She'd attended every day of court so far, but we hadn't spoken. She was staying in the old house, Brian had said, while she readied it to sell. Even with no one around to contest the will, things were moving slowly. I couldn't believe she'd stay there, after what had happened, but Rebecca had always been the sort of person to set her own feelings aside and get done what needed to be done. I wondered what she must think of me, listening to Patty Sue's testimony. Her opinion of me was already so low I doubted it could go much lower.

Brian had ripped Patty Sue's testimony apart, of course, using her own words against her, demanding to know how she'd been able to identify blood from the inside of a car in the *pitch dark* of the river bottoms. She'd had no good explanation for that, other than that she *just knew*, which Brian reminded her with obvious incredulity wouldn't hold up in a court of law.

It could just as easily have been mud, couldn't it?

No sir. It could not. It was blood. I just know it.

How do you know it? Did you have it tested? Did you see it in your crystal ball?

Mr. McDonald's objection was sustained, of course, and Brian received a warning. He could be a bit of a smartass in court, I was learning, and I rather liked it. "We won that round," he said, seemingly unperturbed as the guards took my elbows to lead me back to my cell. "If that's the best they've got, we have nothing to worry about."

"Brian," I said, as I was pulled to the door. "We need to talk."

"We'll have plenty of time in the morning."

"I don't think you understand. If Patty Sue saw me—"

"Lena!" The harshness of his tone startled me. "I'll meet you back at the jail," he said, his voice lower but no less harsh, "and we can talk then. What we won't do is talk here. Understand? You're going to have to trust me."

The problem was, I didn't. I didn't trust *anyone*, how could I possibly trust this man I barely knew, a man who lived in a completely different world than the one I inhabited? Hell, his *shoes* would have brought enough money on the black market down in the bottoms to buy me food for a year. He couldn't possibly relate to me, or my life, or my choices. He always spent our time jotting notes and nodding and pacing, and the whole endeavor left me feeling as if I were somehow wasting his time. He didn't seem real. He seemed … I don't even know how to explain it. He seemed plastic, like a mannequin. As if he were mimicking what a good attorney should look like, but was hollow beneath the surface.

I'd barely arrived back at the jail when I was hustled to the visiting room. Brian was already there, and he looked as frustrated as I felt, but this time I wouldn't be shushed and interrupted. I'd had enough of that treatment. I was upset, and I planned to let him know it.

"Lena, what the hell—"

"No." This time, I was the one to interrupt. He tilted his head toward me, eyebrows raised, but I forged ahead before he could stop me. "Every time I try to speak to you about my doubts, about the nightmares I've been having, you shut me down. I need you to listen to me. It's my life that's on the line, after all."

"My job is to save you," he said, "it's not to dissect your subconscious memories and interpret your dreams. I'm an attorney, not a psychoanalyst. I've been down that road before, and I won't go down it again. That's what Dr. Lewis is for."

"Oh, just shut it," I said, and felt a small thrill when his eyes widened in apparent surprise. "You breeze in and out with your fancy haircut, curls arranged just so. You spend a fortune to get those curls like that, don't you? You with your polished nails, acting like you're better than I am, like you don't have time to listen to me, but you know what? We're the ones paying for those pretty suits. You wouldn't be anything if it weren't for people like me, so sit your prissy ass down and listen for a minute."

To my surprise, he sat, mumbling something under his breath.

"You need to say something?" For the first time in months, I finally felt as if I had some power. I was going to enjoy it while I could.

"Buffed," he said, shifting in his seat. "They're buffed. Not polished." He held up his hand, wiggling his fingers in front of my face. "I'm not *that* pretentious."

The insanity of the situation tickled me, and I laughed.

"Glad I could amuse you," he said, his own lips turning up in a smile. "Now, what can I do for you, Lena? You seem a little miffed."

Now that I had his attention, I wasn't sure where to start. "There's so much evidence against me," I said. "The handprints. Patty Sue. My history with my parents."

"We've never claimed you had anything but a contentious relationship with your parents," Brian reminded me. "We've never said you weren't there. We've said you didn't kill your parents. Remember my opening statement? 'Lena was there, at the scene of the crime,'" he quoted himself. "'The evidence is indisputable. But Lena was not the one who killed her parents. We will present evidence to show that Lena was drugged and taken there against her will.' Be patient, Lena. It's not our turn yet."

I remembered his statement, of course, but I couldn't fathom how he planned to tie it all together. "But how did I get there? They lived a long way from the bottoms, Brian. Too far to walk."

"That's why we need to find Willie G."

"He didn't have a car," I said. "He was homeless, a bottom-dweller like the rest of us."

"How do you know that? You don't even know his real name. The fact is, Lena, you took drugs from a man you knew nothing about. You passed out in front of a man you knew nothing about. You know, or at least assume, he raped you during that time. Someone certainly did. You have no way of knowing what else he may have done."

He had a point, but I had my doubts. "What if I did it, Brian?"

"You didn't," he said. "You had no injuries, at least none consistent with the crime scene. We have a doctor ready to testify that based on your size, you physically couldn't have inflicted the sorts of wounds they had. Think about it, Lena. Your muscles weren't even sore the next day. You couldn't have done it."

"But the dreams," I said. "They're so vivid. More like memories."

"So what? Even if they *are* memories—and Dr. Lewis believes they are—all it proves is you were there, which we already know. You've never seen yourself with a weapon in these dreams. If you really want to help, stop beating yourself up for something you didn't do, and try to see who's with you. That's what we need to know."

God knew I *had* tried. I'd even agreed to hypnosis, but as Brian well knew, I'd been labeled unsusceptible. I'd even been given a test of sorts, the Stanford

Hypnotic Susceptibility Scale. "It makes sense if you think about it, Lena," Dr. Lewis had said as we went over the results. "You operate at a level of alertness most of us rarely experience. It's paramount to your survival. You rebel, either consciously or subconsciously, at the thought of relinquishing control."

Maybe so, but those particular survival skills were working against me at the moment. No matter how hard I tried to see otherwise, the only faces inhabiting my nightmares were those of my murdered family members.

"Why am I unable to see, Brian? If someone else was there, if someone *took* me there, why can't I see them?"

"That's a question for Dr. Lewis," he said, shrugging. "I imagine she'd say you've suppressed some memories due to the trauma. Me, I'd say you were stoned off your ass."

"I can see why you refuse to play psychoanalyst," I said, amused. He could be funny, I was learning, when he wasn't being a prig.

"I'm definitely better at playing attorney."

"Do you believe Patty Sue saw me with blood on my arms?"

"I think it's quite likely."

"Then why did you make a fool of her in court today?"

"I didn't make a fool of her. She made a fool of herself. You can't just waltz into court and make things up. She had no way of knowing that was blood. She later heard about the murders and made an assumption. That's not the same as proof. I wouldn't be doing my job if I didn't call her on it."

"It seemed awfully cruel," I said. "She used to bring us food. Fried apple pies. Some weeks, her pies were all I had."

"What happened in court today doesn't take away from the kindness she's shown you in the past, Lena. She was being honest and doing her civic duty by being there and reporting what she believes she saw. I was doing mine by cross-examining her. That's the way it works." He sat back, regarding me. "You don't like me much, do you?"

"Not really," I said. I'd never been one to mince words. "You're arrogant. Full of yourself. You don't want to win because you believe in your clients' innocence; you want to win because you like winning. You want to own the persona."

"Persona," he said, smiling. "That's a good word."

"I'm not stupid, Brian."

"That's not what I mean. I just have a thing for words, always have. Persona is a good one. I don't hear it very often."

I rolled my eyes. "Whatever. My point is I need to feel as though you're invested in this case beyond a paycheck. I don't appreciate being talked over and pushed aside. You're not a better person than I am, Brian, in spite of your manicure, and I'm more than a means to your next Gucci suit."

"My mother was a drug addict," he said, and this time it was my eyes that widened in surprise. "I was shuffled through foster homes. Didn't know my father. Won a football scholarship, then lost it and nearly flunked out of college. Would have, had I not become friends with a couple of wonderful people. They saved my life, really. There's more to me than you see, Lena. You used the word *persona*. You're right. It's a façade, carefully constructed to win, not because I simply like winning, although I do prefer it, but because I know my clients. I identify with them. There but for the grace of God, and all that. You don't want me to judge you based on what little I know of you. Fair enough. How about you extend me the same courtesy?"

Maybe it was the harsh light; maybe it was something else. Whatever the reason, I noticed for the first time how tired he looked. It couldn't be easy, defending the worst of the worst. If I'd been a different sort of person, I'd have been moved by his vulnerability. But I'm Lena. "Deal," I said with a shrug of my own.

"Are we good, then?" he asked, reaching for his briefcase.

"We're cool."

"In that case, I'll see you in the morning." He stood and walked to the door, turning back to me before he exited. "Those wonderful people I mentioned? One of them was excellent at putting me in my place when she felt I'd gotten too big for my britches. She's no longer here. Thanks for stepping in to pick up her slack."

He left with a wave, and I was taken back to my cell to spend the night tossing and turning as my cellmate snored her way through what I hoped were happy dreams.

Chapter 21: Trial Transcript

Defense Attorney: Dr. Long, what is your role with the Owensfield Police Department?

Dr. Hugh Long: I am a general practitioner, and also a trained forensic examiner. In the rare cases it's needed, I work with the Owensfield Police Department to conduct a physical examination of the suspect of a specific crime.

Defense Attorney: Were you called to assist on the evening of July 18, 2015?

Dr. Hugh Long: I was. I was asked to conduct a physical examination of Lena Reynolds.

Defense Attorney: Did Ms. Reynolds consent to that examination?

Dr. Hugh Long: She did.

Defense Attorney: Dr. Long, I'm showing you a document that's been marked as Defendant's Exhibit A for Identification. Do you recognize this document?

Dr. Hugh Long: It's the consent form signed by Ms. Reynolds.

Defense Attorney: Your Honor, we'd ask that Defendant's Exhibit A for Identification be entered as Defendant's #3.

The Court: Any objections Mr. McDonald?

Prosecutor: No, Your Honor.

The Court: Defendant's Exhibit A will be entered as Defendant's #3.

Defense Attorney: And did you conduct that examination?

Dr. Hugh Long: I did, in my office at approximately 7:00 p.m.

Defense Attorney: Dr. Long, this document has been marked as Defendant's Exhibit B for Identification. Do you recognize this report?

Dr. Hugh Long: I do. It's the post-examination report I submitted to the Owensfield Police Department.

Defense Attorney: Does this report include photographs of any wounds you found on the defendant?

Dr. Hugh Long: Yes, it does.

Defense Attorney: Your Honor, we'd ask that Defendant's Exhibit B be entered as Defendant's #4.

The Court: Mr. McDonald?

Prosecutor: No objections, Your Honor.

The Court: Very well. Defendant's Exhibit B will be entered as Defendant's #4. Continue, Mr. Stone.

Defense Attorney: Did your physical examination of Ms. Reynolds find any wounds on her body?

Dr. Hugh Long: Yes, it did.

Defense Attorney: What were those wounds?

Dr. Hugh Long: She had long scratch marks on her forearms, three on the left arm, and two on the right.

Defense Attorney: Were those marks consistent with fingernail scratches?

Dr. Hugh Long: In my opinion, no. They were more consistent with marks that may have been left by branches or thorns.

Defense Attorney: On what do you base that opinion?

Dr. Hugh Long: They were very thin scratches, very narrow, approximately one millimeter wide, ranging from six to ten inches in length. As you can see in the photographs, they did not run parallel. That is to say, they weren't placed side-by-side on the arm as one would see with fingernail marks. In addition, there were two thorns embedded in the deepest scratch mark on her left arm, and there was one thorn partially embedded in the deeper of the two scratches on her right arm.

Defense Attorney: Were there any other wounds on her body?

Dr. Hugh Long: There were abrasions in the vaginal area. Two were healing. One appeared to be fresh.

Defense Attorney: Would the abrasions have been consistent with what you might see in a rape victim?

Prosecutor: Objection. Irrelevant to the case at hand.

The Court: I'll allow it, Mr. McDonald, as it falls without the argument set forth in Defense's opening statements. You may answer the question, Dr. Long.

Dr. Hugh Long: It's impossible to say. I have seen abrasions such as these in cases of rape, but I've also seen them during standard pelvic exams in which the patient was unaware she had them.

Defense Attorney: Did you record any other wounds during your exam of Ms. Reynolds?

Dr. Hugh Long: Yes. Ms. Reynolds had noticeable bruising on each knee, right in the front, where the patella would be. They were deep purple in color, indicating they were several days old. The bruise on her left knee measured four centimeters across. The bruise on the right knee was larger, measuring just over five centimeters and covering nearly the entire surface of the knee.

Defense Attorney: Would those bruises be consistent with falling to one's knees?

Dr. Hugh Long: Yes, I'd say they'd be very consistent with that.

Defense Attorney: Were there other injuries?

Dr. Hugh Long: Ms. Reynolds had a long scrape mark on the outside of her left thigh.

Defense Attorney: What sort of scrape mark, Dr. Long?

Dr. Hugh Long: It measured thirty centimeters from hip to knee. At the hip, it measured nine centimeters wide, narrowing to three centimeters at the knee.

Defense Attorney: What could cause a scrape such as that?

Dr. Hugh Long: I most often see a wound like that on someone who fell and slid, or was dragged, over some distance. It's the sort of wound one associates with carpet burn or road rash.

Defense Attorney: Dr. Long, did the defendant remember acquiring any of those wounds?

Dr. Hugh Long: No, she did not.

Defense Attorney: Were there any other wounds?

Dr. Hugh Long: No.

Defense Attorney: No cuts or incisions?

Dr. Hugh Long: No, nothing else.

Defense Attorney: Did Ms. Reynolds complain of muscle pain or stiffness?

Dr. Hugh Long: She did not, and her reflexes and range of motion were all within the normal range.

Defense Attorney: How tall is Ms. Reynolds, Doctor?

Dr. Hugh Long: Ms. Reynolds stands at five feet, three inches and weighs 120 pounds.

Defense Attorney: I believe you also submitted lab work, did you not? A blood test? Fingernail scrapings?

Dr. Hugh Long: I did.

Defense Attorney: I'm holding what's been marked as Defendant's Exhibit C for Identification in my hand. Do you recognize it?

Dr. Hugh Long: I do. It's the report I received from the lab.

Defense Attorney: Your Honor, we'd ask that Defendant's Exhibit C be entered as Defendant's #5.

The Court: Any objections?

Prosecutor: No, Your Honor.

The Court: Defendant's Exhibit C will be entered as Defendant's #5. Continue, please.

Defense Attorney: Did the lab find any evidence of drugs in Ms. Reynolds' lab specimen?

Dr. Hugh Long: Yes. Ms. Reynolds tested positive for a small amount of Demerol.

Defense Attorney: You said "a small amount." Can you explain the half-life of Demerol, and tell us the significance of the amount measured?

Prosecutor: Objection. Dr. Long is a well-respected physician, but I'm unaware of any credentials that qualify him to explain the lab results in the detail my colleague requests.

The Court: Sustained. Move on, Mr. Stone.

Defense Attorney: Moving right along. We'll leave that question for my next witness.

The Court: Just continue, Mr. Stone, with this witness.

Defense Attorney: I have no further questions for this witness, Your Honor.

The Court: Your witness, Mr. McDonald. Let's see if we can keep things on track.

Chapter 22: Brian Stone

I WAS STARTLED by an unexpected knock on my office door. It was Sunday morning, early, and I'd stopped by to pick up some notes I'd neglected to bring home in my briefcase. I hadn't expected anyone, not on a Sunday, and I was dressed accordingly: old jeans; a long-sleeved, royal blue University of Memphis t-shirt; and top-siders.

"May I come in?" Rebecca asked. I removed my glasses and waved her in. "Sorry to bother you," she said as she took a seat in front of my desk. "I had to come to town to get some plumbing fixtures. It's a mess out there, and you know Owensfield. Nothing's open on Sundays, and even if it were, it wouldn't have what I need."

"Makes me have second thoughts about moving to the country," I said with a smile. I'd enjoyed talking with Rebecca the few times I'd had the opportunity. She was smart, composed. Friendly, in a distant sort of way.

"Don't do it," she advised now. "Take the money and run." She returned my smile.

"Has it been awful?"

She sighed, leaning back in the chair. "They just have so much stuff. Farm equipment, canning jars, old issues of *Reader's Digest* and *National Geographic*. Boxes and boxes of old blankets and quilts, most with either moth holes or mouse nests. I have an auction scheduled for next weekend. Hopefully that'll take care of some of it. Goodwill will pick up anything worthwhile that doesn't sell, and I'll haul the rest to the dump."

"Is there nothing you want?"

She shook her head. "I'm sure you've learned by now Lena and I don't have the best memories of the old place. How is she, by the way?"

"Why don't you stop by and visit? You're on the list. I can give them a call while you're in town."

"No." She shook her head. "It's better this way. I'll show my support by attending the trial. We're always better at a distance. We wouldn't last five minutes without fighting if we were alone in the same room." She scooted forward. "Did she do it, Brian? Lawyer talk aside, do you believe she did it? I really need to know."

"Even if I did believe it, I certainly wouldn't tell you," I said, "but as it happens, I don't believe she did. I think someone took her there. There's the missing safe, remember?"

"But it never had much in it, in the way of money."

"'Not much' is relative. What isn't much to you could be a fortune to someone she knew from the bottoms."

"True," she said. "To think someone would commit that sort of crime for a few hundred dollars …" She shivered.

"I've seen worse."

"I'm sure you have," she said. "I don't see how you maintain your sunny outlook." I caught a hint of sarcasm in her tone.

"It isn't always easy."

"I'm sure. Well," she said, standing, "I'll get out of your hair. I just really needed to know if you thought Lena …" she broke off. "What's that? Why do you have a drawing of William?"

She was pointing to a composite drawing of Willie G. that sat on the pile of papers I'd come to retrieve. We'd had it done shortly after Lena's arrest, as I began piecing her story together and realized he held the key to everything. "William?" I straightened, on high alert. "What do you know about this man?"

"That's William Wells. William Garrett Wells, as he introduced himself to me. I remember, because I thought it was odd he mentioned his middle name. Most people don't. He used to do work for my father. Handyman stuff. I think Dad met him at the food pantry at church a couple of years ago. Dad got to know him, liked him, and started hiring him for odd jobs around the farm, stuff Dad finally understood I physically just couldn't do. He cut down a couple of trees, leveled the gravel drive. I met him a few times when I was there. He used to bring my parents fried pies made by his wife from the apples on our farm. They were delicious. They were always in a cardboard box along with a bunch of religious pamphlets. The pamphlets are still there, in a stack of junk on the kitchen counter. One more thing I have to get rid of. Why? What does he have to do with any of this?"

I was on my feet by then. "This is Willie G., the man we've been looking for. The one who drugged Lena to the extent she has no memory of what happened during the time of the murders. You mean to tell me you *know* this guy? That he's married to the woman I cross-examined just days ago? There can't be two evangelical fried pie makers in this town."

"You'd be surprised," she said. "But yes, I know this guy."

"Damn, Rebecca, do you know how hard we've worked to find someone, anyone, who could tell us who he is? I can't believe it's you. This is amazing!"

"I'm sorry Brian, but I had no idea. I'd never heard him referred to as Willie G., and I didn't know that woman was his wife. I didn't make the connection between their names. Wells is a fairly common name, and I'd never met her, just William. What's the significance of this? What are you thinking?"

"Don't you see? This is brilliant. It's the answer to everything. Willie G.—William Garrett Wells, as you know him—had inside access to your family. He knew the layout of the house, possibly even where the safe was kept. He would have had some idea of their financial status. He's the one who drugged Lena the day of the murder, for God's sake. Was his wife involved? Did he seek Lena out after meeting your family? Or did he know Lena first?" I was pacing, wheels turning. "Where is he now?"

"I don't know the answers to any of those questions," Rebecca said. "I never even knew where he lived, just that he came by every so often to do work for my dad. I can look through Dad's desk again, see if there's something I missed. I wouldn't have paid attention to anything mentioning William the first few times, nor would have the cops, because we didn't realize he was significant."

"Significant? Rebecca, he's *everything*. He's the man who set your sister up."

Chapter 23: Trial Transcript

Defense Attorney: It's good to see you again, Mrs. Wells.

Patty Sue Wells: Thank you, sir. It's good to see you, too. I forgive you for last time. The Lord teaches us to forgive, and I do what the Lord tells me to do.

Defense Attorney: I appreciate that, Mrs. Wells. When you were called by the prosecution as a witness, you testified that you saw the defendant, Lena Reynolds, walking down Bucktail Road at 3 o'clock the morning of July 14, 2015. Is that correct?

Patty Sue Wells: Yes, sir. That's what I saw.

Defense Attorney: What is your husband's name, Mrs. Wells?

Patty Sue Wells: William Garrett Wells, but his friends call him Willie G.

Defense Attorney: Was your husband with you in the car the morning of July 14?

Patty Sue Wells: No, sir. He was not.

Defense Attorney: When was the last time you had seen him before that morning?

Patty Sue Wells: I haven't seen Willie G in nigh about a year. He left me last spring. May, I believe it was. I asked him for money to pay the electric and he got mad. He'd drunk it all up, you see. Always did, leaving me to pay everything from my disability, which ain't hardly enough to live on. Anyway, he left. Slammed the door on his way out. I ain't seen him since.

Defense Attorney: I want to make sure I understand. Your husband left two months before the murder of the Reynolds family took place?

Patty Sue Wells: That's right.

Defense Attorney: And you haven't seen him since?

Patty Sue Wells: I have not.

Defense Attorney: Do you know where he was for those two months?

Patty Sue Wells: Not for sure, no. I assumed he went somewhere down in the bottoms.

Prosecutor: Objection. The witness is speculating.

The Court: Sustained.

Defense Attorney: I'll rephrase the question, Your Honor. Mrs. Wells, did Mr. Wells have a particular place he liked to go when he was angry with you?

Patty Sue Wells: He did. He'd go drinking down in the bottoms, hanging out with the riff-raff.

Defense Attorney: Can you tell me what you mean when you say, "the bottoms"?

Patty Sue Wells: Down by the river. Off Bucktail Road.

Defense Attorney: Thank you. Mrs. Wells, did you know Eugene and Becky Reynolds?

Patty Sue Wells: No, sir. I've heard since all this happened that Mr. Reynolds used to be the mayor, but that would have been before we got here. We came here from Texas in two thousand eleven. He was retired by then, from what I understand.

Defense Attorney: You never met Mr. and Mrs. Reynolds?

Patty Sue Wells: No, sir. Not that I know of.

Defense Attorney: Ever hear your husband talk about them?

Patty Sue Wells: Not by name, no.

Defense Attorney: What do you mean, not by name?

Patty Sue Wells: I mean, I knew he did some work for someone just outside town from time to time. Rich man, he said. Met him at the food pantry a couple of years ago. Willie G. went there looking for fresh fruit for my pies. Said one of the men working there had apple trees on his farm and invited Willie G. out to get some. It was shortly after that Willie G. started doing some work for him.

Defense Attorney: I've heard your pies are wonderful.

Patty Sue Wells: Thank you, sir. I'd be happy to bring you some.

Defense Attorney: That's quite all right, Mrs. Wells, but I appreciate the offer. Now, back to your husband. You knew he did odd jobs for a rich family outside of town. You now know that was the Reynolds family?

Patty Sue Wells: Yes, sir.

Defense Attorney: But when you were previously questioned, you never mentioned your husband had worked for them. Why is that?

Patty Sue Wells: Why, no one asked, and the judge here kept telling me to stick to the questions.

Defense Attorney: All right, then. Mrs. Wells, did Mr. Wells ever tell you the rich family he worked for had a daughter they'd disowned?

Patty Sue Wells: He did. He said she'd given her daddy a terrible time.

Defense Attorney: Did Mr. Wells ever mention where the disowned daughter lived?

Patty Sue Wells: No, sir. Not that I remember.

Defense Attorney: He never mentioned she lived down in the bottoms?

Patty Sue Wells: No, sir.

Defense Attorney: You're sure about that?

Prosecutor: Objection. Asked and answered.

The Court: Sustained.

Defense Attorney: No more questions. Thank you, Mrs. Wells.

Chapter 24: Rebecca

I WAS WORKING hard to dispel my anger, but I wasn't having much luck. I'd spent so much time in Owensfield my job was in jeopardy—and by extension, my apartment—but there was just no way to take care of it all from four hours away. Probate, the trial, the land, the house, the junk. It had consumed my life. If I'd thought my family encroached upon my life before their deaths, I was in for a rude awakening after.

My supervisor had been as supportive as I could have hoped for, but here I was, ten months into this mess, with no signs of it letting up. I'd taken off nearly as many days the past few months as I'd worked. He'd done all he could to support me; I couldn't ask for more, and I knew he couldn't give it. Ultimately, I decided to hand in my resignation and give up my apartment, moving into my parents' house and hoping like hell I could at least sell enough of their junk on eBay to survive until everything was settled. It was the last place I wanted to be, but I had no choice.

You'll have plenty, my father had always said whenever I'd expressed my concerns regarding his estate planning. *Just sell the land.* That was easier said than done. I still didn't have the okay to sell it, and besides, there was no guarantee it would sell. Owensfield isn't exactly a thriving metropolis. My best hope was one of the local farmers, maybe even the family who'd rented it for the past few years. But from what I could see, they were barely scraping by. Farm land is priced comparatively low, but given the struggles faced by small farmers, maybe not low enough. Meanwhile, I was getting bills from the funeral home, and property taxes were past due. Debts were piling up, and I had no way to pay them.

Brian wanted me to search for anything that had to do with Willie G., but how in the hell was I supposed to find anything in the chaos my father had called an office? There were boxes and binders and piles of papers. I'd gone through everything months ago when looking for bills and deeds and necessary information, but the thought of sorting through it all again was enough to send me over the edge.

I was overwhelmed, sitting on the floor in the midst of a major tantrum, fan blowing in an attempt to stem the sweat, when I heard a tapping on the window. I looked up to see Brian Stone, looking as cool as ever in a polo shirt, motioning me toward the kitchen to open the back door.

"Jesus, it's like an oven in here," he said, stepping inside and pushing silver curls off his forehead. "It's hotter in here than it is out there."

"I'm conserving energy," I said, struggling to keep my anger under control. "I can't afford to pay for air-conditioning. They've left me in quite a jam."

"I'm sorry to hear that," he said, swiping an arm across his forehead. "How can you stand it?"

"There's nothing I can do about it. Unlike you, I can't leave." I knew my answer was rude, but I didn't need Brian reminding me how unbearable my situation was.

"I thought maybe you could use some help looking through your dad's stuff," he said.

"Your caseload is that light?"

"Lena is my only client at the moment. Anyway, I've got a couple of witnesses who'll testify they saw Willie G. and Lena together during that time period, one who claims to have sold him enough Demerol July thirteenth to choke a horse—I've spent a fun morning down in the bottoms—but if we could find Willie G., that would be icing on the cake."

"I can only imagine the reception you got down in the bottoms," I said, the thought of Brian in his meticulously pressed jeans wandering along the riverbank nearly making me laugh. "Glad you made it out in one piece, and glad you have some witnesses. Why in the world would anyone admit selling drugs to Willie G.?"

"The dealer is already in jail. Got busted a few weeks ago for selling drugs to an undercover officer. His name kept coming up, so I followed the gossip trail and found him sitting behind bars."

"So he's trying to cut a deal."

Brian shrugged. "Maybe. But his story is credible."

"I hope so," I said. "I guess we'll see. And thanks for coming by. I'd appreciate the help. It's going to be tough to find anything in this clutter." I led him down the dark hallway and into the office. "Your defense of

Lena is obviously that William is the one who killed them. If that's the case, I'm not sure anything we find could be of much help. He's going to be motivated to remain out of sight, and he and my dad had a working relationship. He certainly wouldn't have confided in my dad about his secret hiding places."

"I'm sure you're right, but we have to look. At the very least, we should be able to find something that proves he knew your parents and had access to inside information. Cancelled checks proving he'd been paid by your dad, notations on a calendar regarding when work was scheduled. Anything. You never know what might be relevant. Hell, I wouldn't have thought in a million years your William Garrett was Lena's Willie G. And yes, I do believe he killed them. I think he drugged Lena and used her to gain entry, then staged the crime scene to make it appear she'd killed your family."

"There's just one problem with your theory," I said. "William wouldn't have needed Lena to gain entry. My parents knew and trusted him. If he'd come knocking on their door in the middle of the night, they would have assumed he needed help and let him in. I'm not sure they'd have done the same for Lena."

"Things were that bad between them?" He didn't sound surprised.

"Let's just say they'd had their fill of Lena knocking on the door in the middle of the night with some emergency or other. Whether she was hiding from the cops or from someone else or just needed money, they stopped opening the door to Lena ages ago, shortly after a friend of hers forced his way in and locked them in their bedroom while he made off with my mother's silver and my father's guns."

"You don't think they'd softened over the years?"

"It's not just that they hadn't softened, it's that they wouldn't have trusted her. Sad, isn't it? They wouldn't have opened the door to their own daughter. But she earned that reputation, both by her own actions and by the company she kept. This is a perfect example, if you think about it. You believe there's a connection between Lena and William, and you also believe William killed my family. He's exactly the sort of person Lena's always been drawn to. They were afraid of her, of her friends, her inability to make good choices, and their fears were proven valid once again, this time in the worst sort of way. Here, you take this box. I'll go through the desk again."

"Maybe you're right," he said, "but from everything I can find, your parents knew William before William knew Lena. If anything, it sounds to me as if your parents led William to Lena, instead of the other way around. Your parents weren't William's only victims, you know. He victimized Lena, too, and I don't just mean by framing her as a murderer." He took the box and settled onto the worn carpet to begin his search.

"Lena victimized herself," I said, yanking on a stubborn drawer. That damn drawer had been sticking the entirety of my life. More than once, my father had to screw the handle back in place with toothpicks shoved in the hole to give the stripped-out screw something to grip. "She victimized herself with the life choices she made." I gave an extra hard yank, and wouldn't you know that goddamn handle came off again, scattering toothpick slivers on the floor. It took all my self-control not to throw it across the room. I took a deep breath, struggling to tamp down my temper, not an easy feat with sweat dripping into my eyes.

"Look, Brian," I said, gently setting the handle on the desk and willing my voice to remain steady. "You don't know that they met William first; you're drawing a conclusion with incomplete information. I'd have thought you'd know better. William came to work for my father a couple of years ago and you think, based on his wife's testimony, he may have begun living down in the bottoms a couple of months before my family was killed, during which time he met Lena. And then what? He saw Lena and suddenly decided to kill my family? After William had been happily working for them for two years? That doesn't even make sense."

"It does, though." Brian stood and paced, the box apparently forgotten. "Remember, Patty Sue Wells knew enough about your family to know they'd disowned a daughter, yet Willie G. never mentioned having met the daughter down in the bottoms. Never even indicated he knew where she was. I don't think he did, initially. I think he came across Lena during one of his drunken forays after a fight with his wife, and once he made the connection, began to hatch a plan. A damn good one, if you think about it. He knew there was bad blood between Lena and your parents. Who better to pin the murder on?"

I shook my head, turning my attention to another drawer. "Still doesn't make sense. Why now? Why, period? Think of it this way: his wife said he had a habit of drinking with men down in the bottoms whenever they fought. Lena has been living down there for years. What if he met Lena first, years ago, and she led him to our family? What if he's been working the last couple of years to gain my parents' trust? That sounds more plausible to me than your theory does."

"'Why now' has the same answer as 'why period.' Because he needed money." He sat again, pulling the box close. "Patty Sue testified that was the cause of their last fight, remember? She needed money for the electric bill, and they fought because he'd spent it all on booze. They fought, he left, met Lena, and a plan was hatched."

"And you think in his boozed-up, drugged-out state he came up with the idea to butcher my family and make Lena the fall guy, all just to pay the electric bill? Sounds a little complicated for a drunk. Besides, Lena has a long history as a master manipulator. She's had decades of practice. If one of them manipulated the other, my money is on Lena."

"Not 'just' to pay the electric bill. For all he knew, there were thousands in that safe. And as I've told you before, what's paltry to some is wealth to others. You have so little compassion," he said, studying me as if I were a foreign object, an altogether displeasing one. "Do you understand the things she's been through all these years, the myriad ways she's been hurt?"

"Does she understand the ways she's hurt everyone else?" My temper flared again. I felt like a shit for stubbornly refusing to recognize Lena's pain, but she wasn't the only one who'd been hurt, dammit, and while I *hadn't* been the one to hurt her, she *had* been the one to hurt me. I was tired of Lena's claim on victimhood.

"You seem to be trying awfully hard to convince me Lena is guilty," he said. "Why?"

"Because I think she is," I said, and he stopped his sorting, holding a sheaf of papers in midair.

"You say that so matter-of-factly." He set the papers down, his attention focused on me instead. He really was a handsome man, even with sweat beaded on his forehead and spreading underneath his arm-pits. Too bad he was such a prig.

"It's something I've thought a lot about," I said, setting down my own stack of papers. "I know my sister, Brian. Excuses could be made for her when she was young. She had a shitty childhood, no doubt about it. She spent years punishing my parents for it and me right along with them. She steals and lies and threatens. She even stole my identity once, did she tell you that? No? You should ask her about it sometime. It took years for me to get it sorted out, and even now if you Google my name you'll be stunned at what pops up. I had to change phone numbers to get the bottom-dwellers to stop calling me.

"She tried to do it again just weeks before my family was killed. She stole my credit card number. I don't even know how she got it, but she ran the card up so high I'll be paying it off for years, and she didn't have a damn thing to show for it when I caught her. But here I sit sweating my ass off, too poor to run the air-conditioner.

"I have no job, no apartment, all because of whom? Lena. Again. You know what? I didn't even press charges the last time. What's the point? There's no end to what Lena will do. After some of the stunts she's pulled, murder just seems like the next step in the process. I imagine I'll be next. Bill hinted as much. If she doesn't do it all at once, she'll just keep chipping away at my life until I no longer have one.

At this point, I don't even care." I opened another drawer, angrily dumping out the contents and combing through them, struggling to catch my breath after my unexpected diatribe. "Your turn," I said, when I could breathe normally again. "You're so convinced she *didn't* do it. Why?"

"That was quite a story," he said quietly, still watching me. "I can see why you're so angry, and I'm sorry. Maybe I see a different side of her because she's new to me. You have years of baggage to deal with. Bad memories, family history. You've experienced a Lena I never have and never will. My relationship with Lena began with a clean slate. The woman I've come to know isn't nearly as tough as she thinks she is. She uses anger to protect herself. Now I'm starting to sound like Dr. Lewis, but it's true. Underneath it all, I see a hurt little girl. What I don't see is a murderer."

"At some point that hurt little girl has to grow up," I said. "She can't use that excuse forever. Everyone has shit they have to deal with. There comes a time when you have to get over it and move on."

"Those wounds run deep," he countered. "You know that yourself. Lena wears her anger right on the surface, but yours isn't far below. You just deal with it differently. Lena feels out of control so that's what she presents to the world. You feel out of control so you work hard to control the world."

"Kind of presumptuous, aren't you?" I hated my sharp tone, but I seemed powerless to stop it. "I hadn't realized you doubled as a psychotherapist. And still with only the one client. Interesting."

"I don't mean to be presumptuous, but I'm no stranger to wrecked childhoods. I had one of my own. I recognize another damaged child when I see one."

I sat silently, absorbing what he'd just said. It was unexpected, catching me off guard and effectively quashing my agitation. If he'd meant to knock me off my pedestal, he'd succeeded. Maybe I hadn't given him enough credit. It made sense, what he'd said, but a small part of me resented not only his presumed familiarity, but also his total acceptance of Lena's innocence.

Lena had made my life hell in so many ways. Did I think she had it in her to kill my parents? Sure, under the right circumstances. Doesn't *everyone* have it within themselves to commit murder, under the right circumstances? I'd certainly had times I felt like killing Lena. I believe we're all capable of those impulses, whether we'd like to admit it or not. It's just that most of us don't put ourselves in situations to allow the impulses to come to fruition. But Lena put herself in terrible situations over and over again. It had become difficult, over the years, to see her as a victim.

Even as I resented his acceptance of Lena, I also wished I could give it. I wanted to be able to do that for Lena, and I felt both sorry and guilty that I couldn't. "Look, let's just get this done, okay? We have too much literal garbage to dig through today without adding figurative garbage to the list." I was ready to change subjects; the current one was exhausting. I was hot, my head was pounding, and I just wanted to be done with it all. "It's good Lena has you," I said, and I meant it. "She's lucky."

"There are some days I'm not sure she'd agree," he said with a smile that lightened the atmosphere. "She thinks I'm a prig."

Apparently Lena and I had more in common than I'd thought.

"And for what it's worth, you both have me. Tell you what," he was saying, "is that your dad's truck out there, and if it is, does it still run?" I nodded, and he continued. "Let's pack this stuff into it and go somewhere else. Somewhere with air-conditioning. We could use some cooling down. I'll call and see if maybe we can use a room at the sta—"

He was interrupted by the chirp of his cell even as he'd been pulling it from his pocket. "Speak of the devil," he said, clicking it on and holding it to his ear. "Brian Stone here." A pause. "Good to hear from you, Bill." *Bill Frazier*, he mouthed to me. "I was just on my way there with Rebecca. Why, what's up?" Another pause. "Oh, my God. Please tell me you're joking." I sat and waited, watching the color drain from his face. "I'll be right there. I'll have Rebecca with me; is that okay?" The seconds ticked by. "Of course. Is there a room she can use? We're going through papers … Thanks, Bill. I appreciate it. Give us fifteen minutes." He clicked the phone off and stood, shoving it into his pocket.

"They've found Willie G.," he said, his expression grim. He reached out a hand to help me to my feet.

I was surprised by his reaction to Bill's call. "Why do you seem upset? This is good news, right?"

"Not really," he said, handing me one box and taking two more for himself. "He's dead."

Chapter 25: Lena

I SUPPOSE I should have been sorry about Willie G., but I wasn't. A couple of fishermen found his skeleton just north of the Hatchie Towhead where the Hatchie and Mississippi Rivers meet. DNA testing of the femur confirmed it was him, but the size and gender of the remains, along with the lack of teeth, no doubt helped point them in the right direction. Due to the floods back in January there was no way to know exactly when and where the body entered the water, and if it hadn't gotten caught up in submerged tree branches God only knew where—or if—it would have ever been found.

The Lower Mississippi is notoriously fickle, full of shifting currents and powerful whirlpools. No one agrees on the exact origin of the name, but it's thought to be a Native American word meaning "The Father of Waters." If you've ever been lucky enough to stand on the banks of the Mississippi and watch its power, you'll understand why. Some people think the river is haunted. Others think it's cursed.

If you don't believe me, just ask some of the old timers from Kaskaskia. They'll know the history. Or ask Ancient Joe, down in the bottoms. He's the one who told me. Ancient Joe claims to be descended from the Illiniwek, who he says inhabited almost all of Illinois until the French showed up. I don't know if he really is descended, or if he's delusional. Either way, he knows the history of the Mississippi River Valley better than any historian ever could, and he loves to tell stories.

According to Ancient Joe, it all started in 1735 when a rich white fur trader discovered his lovely young daughter in love with a Native American man. The affair ended with the young man tied to a log and shoved into the river to die. As he drowned he cursed the town, swearing Kaskaskia and all the land around it would be damned.

I don't know how much of that is true, although Ancient Joe swears by it, and how much is just a good story, but in 1881 the Mississippi River changed course and wiped out most of what was at one time the capital of territorial Illinois. It's rumored the dead floated up out of their graves before seeking a final resting place somewhere along the river's bottom.

When all was said and done, Kaskaskia went from being a peninsula attached to Illinois, to an island accessible only by an old bridge connecting it to Missouri. The once thriving metropolis is now mostly a ghost town with just a handful of residents, fourteen at the time of the last census. Ancient Joe says the river was happy to rise up and help the young Illiniwek man because the white people were cutting down all the trees and ruining the land.

I don't know if that's true, either, but my own belief is that the Mississippi is a moody river that doesn't discriminate when it comes to wreaking havoc. In 1927 it spilled over the banks and killed nearly 250 people, displacing over 600,000 more, many of them poor indentured farmers and field workers. It's been called one of the five most dangerous rivers in the world, and some say it's been responsible for more deaths in the U.S. than any other river.

And yet, I love that river. That essay I had to write in fifth grade? The one about a feeling of homesickness? I wrote about the Mississippi River. We'd taken a field trip a few weeks before, an end to a unit on ecosystems, and Ms. Sterling arranged a trip to Shelby Forest so we could stand on the boat dock and see the Mighty Mississippi.

I stood watching the rushing, churning water and felt something I'd never felt before and can scarcely describe. *Awe* is probably the best way to describe it, but that doesn't do it justice. It was electrifying—powerful, unrelenting, unapologetic, and unforgiving. It raised the hair on my neck and sent chills down my spine. It was raw and violent and enthralling. To a young girl who felt utterly powerless, the attraction was irresistible. I knew eventually I'd live by that river. I just hadn't known the circumstances under which I'd do it.

When Brian told me Willie G.'s body had been found tangled in branches at the confluence of the Hatchie and the Mississippi, and that my daddy's axe had been found washed up just half a mile south, I knew it was fate. I'd lived on Old Man River's banks for decades, taking up refuge when my own father locked the door against me and pulled down the shade.

I'd worshipped that river, and now he'd held Willie G. and that axe still for us, just waiting for us to find them. As for how he'd ended up in the river in the first place, no one knew, but Brian and I speculated, given what we knew of his history, he'd been either drunk or stoned and fallen in, maybe as he was attempting to throw away the axe. There was nothing to indicate otherwise—no broken or splintered bones, which was all that was left of him, and either no witnesses, or no witnesses willing to talk. Brian said the investigation into his death had hit a brick wall, and no one seemed particularly concerned with finding a way around it.

"But we're just speculating, Lena, and speculation won't win this case. We're close. We're getting there. We've linked him to the murder weapon, but we need one of two things. We need a witness willing to testify having seen Willie with the axe in hand, or we need to link him to the scene. Both would be even better. We've got to create enough reasonable doubt to make a guilty verdict impossible, and we're not quite there yet."

I understood what Brian was saying, but in my mind the Mississippi River was on my side, and that was almost as good as an acquittal.

Chapter 26: Trial Transcript

Court Clerk: State your name for the record, please.

Thomas Mackenzie: Thomas J. Mackenzie, but you can call me Tommy Mac.

Court Clerk: Spell your last name, please.

Thomas Mackenzie: M-a-c-k-e-n-z-i-e.

The Court: Your witness, Mr. Stone.

Defense Attorney: Good morning, Mr. Mackenzie.

Thomas Mackenzie: Good morning.

Defense Attorney: Mr. Mackenzie, where do you reside?

Thomas Mackenzie: Well, right now I reside in the county jail, but usually I live down in the bottoms. I have a little place down there built out of pallets.

Defense Attorney: Tell us, if you would, what you mean by "the bottoms."

Thomas Mackenzie: The river bottoms. Off Bucktail.

Defense Attorney: Thank you. How long did you live in the bottoms, Mr. Mackenzie?

Thomas Mackenzie: Well, now, that's a hard question to answer. Off and on my whole life, I reckon. My family had a trailer on some land down there, but the government took it away when I was in my teens. That would have been in ninety-nine. I was old enough to make it on my own, by then. Don't know what happened to some of the little ones. I ain't seen them since. I lived by myself in the bottoms for a couple of years before I joined the army. Got out in two thousand five and went right back down there. Always felt like home to me.

Defense Attorney: Mr. Mackenzie, do you have a job down in the bottoms?

Thomas Mackenzie: Well. Sort of.

Defense Attorney: Can you tell us what that job is?

Thomas Mackenzie: I don't know as you could call it a job, really. It ain't legal, anyways. No point in lying about it, me sitting up here in orange and all. I sell drugs. Opiates, heroin. Big market for that stuff these days, you know.

Defense Attorney: I appreciate your honesty, Mr. Mackenzie. Did you know a man called Willie G. down in the bottoms?

Thomas Mackenzie: Yes, sir, I did. One of my biggest customers.

Defense Attorney: Did you know his full, given name?

Thomas Mackenzie: Not back then, no, but I've heard it on the news since then. William Wells. But everyone just called him Willie G.

Defense Attorney: Did you ever sell Demerol to Willie G.?

Thomas Mackenzie: Dillies, yeah. Once. He came asking for it specifically. Called it "juice," I remember, but I knew what he meant.

Defense Attorney: Do you remember the date?

Thomas Mackenzie: I do, because I didn't have any on me. Most of my customers ask for OC. I told him it would take me a couple of days to get it. He said I'd have to hurry, because he needed it by Monday, July 13.

Defense Attorney: Did he say why he needed it on that particular date?

Thomas Mackenzie: Not exactly. Just smiled and said he needed it for a job. I didn't ask questions. You don't ask questions in my business.

Defense Attorney: Did you sell it to him on July 13?

Thomas Mackenzie: Sure did, eight vials just like he asked. A hundred milligrams each. You gotta be careful injecting Dillies. If you ain't used to it, it'll knock your ass right out. Sorry, Judge.

Defense Attorney: How did William Wells pay for the vials, Mr. Mackenzie?

Thomas Mackenzie: Cash. That's all I'll accept. He pulled a big ol' wad of hundreds out of his pocket. I told him he better watch it, or I might take it all from him. I was mostly just giving him a hard time, you know.

Defense Attorney: Did he respond to that?

Thomas Mackenzie: Yes, sir. He laughed. Said what he had in his pocket was nothing compared to what he was about to get. Stupid, talking like that around … well, around someone like me, to tell you the truth.

Defense Attorney: Did he explain what he meant?

Thomas Mackenzie: No, sir. Just laughed. And like I said, I don't ask.

Defense Attorney: Did you see him again after that?

Thomas Mackenzie: No, sir. I ain't seen him since.

Defense Attorney. Thank you, Mr. Mackenzie. No more questions, Your Honor.

Chapter 27: Lena

ONE THING ABOUT being locked up: it gives you a lot of time to think about things. Too much, really. One of the things I'd spent time thinking about was Willie G. At least that's where the thoughts began, but they ended up in all sorts of places.

Willie G. had sex with me—raped me, as Brian had said—while I was passed out. I assumed it was Willie G. Even if it hadn't been him, he'd left me sprawled out on the riverbank for any and every asshole passing by to use and abuse, and someone had. And that wasn't the first time, either. What does it say about me that *raped* wasn't the first word that came to mind when I regained consciousness on that riverbank, covered with flies, my knees splayed open? It's an ugly picture, isn't it? Well, that's been my life. Finding myself in that predicament, or one like it, wasn't outside the norm. Over the years I guess I'd come to think I deserved that kind of treatment, but the longer I sat in that jail cell, the more I began to wonder.

Does anyone deserve that kind of treatment? I suppose the answer should be obvious, but it wasn't to me. Until quiet time in that cell, the longest I've ever spent in jail, I didn't question my life, didn't question what happened to me or what people did. I don't think I'd ever had the luxury of questioning. I'd spent the bulk of my life reacting, with no thought to planning. When Brian Stone pointed out to me that what Willie G.—or someone—had done was rape, I saw the disgust in his expression. The disgust itself didn't surprise me; I was used to that look. What surprised me was that it wasn't directed at *me*, it was directed at Willie G. He didn't blame me, only Willie G. That was a new experience for me.

As I sat and looked back over my life, not only my adulthood, but my childhood, I began to think maybe I'd deserved better.

Don't get me wrong. I'll be the first to admit I've been a real asshole to people who at one time cared about me. What I mean by that is I've been a real asshole to Rebecca. Rebecca loved me, years ago. She resented me, sure. Why wouldn't she? She couldn't go anywhere or do anything because she always had Callie and me to take care of. But underneath all the anger, she loved us both. I'm sure she did—keyword being *did*.

I thought about Rebecca a lot during the long days court wasn't in session. I'd loved Rebecca, too. I don't know why I'd been such an ass to her. She was the only one who'd ever treated me decently, and I'd repaid her by doing everything I could to disrupt her life. *Why?*

"You were testing," Dr. Lewis said. They'd allowed us to have our session on the roof that day, and

I sat with my face turned to the sky, enjoying the warmth of the sun. I wasn't used to being indoors, much less to being pinned up. I'd dig as deep as Dr. Lewis wanted if it meant she'd stay longer and keep me out of that cell.

"You didn't trust her love," she was saying, "so you tested it constantly. You subconsciously wanted to know how much you could get away with before she abandoned you."

"I'd say the stolen identity part was her limit," I said. "She was angry with me before, but she was finished with me after that."

"That was a big breach of trust," Dr. Lewis said, apparently thinking that was somehow helpful. Nothing like stating the obvious. Dr. Lewis was paid by the court to work with me, or at least I assumed that was who paid her. She'd been assigned for nearly every crime I'd committed the last decade, taking the place of whoever sat in the chair before her. I'd been through half a dozen or so over the years. I don't know where the legal system got the money, or what the specific program was, but whenever a therapist made a pointless statement like the one she'd just made—which happened with some regularity—I wondered if they realized they didn't always get their money's worth.

"I may have been testing her," I said, "but I resented her, too, maybe as much as she resented me. My parents put too much responsibility on her, but at least they acknowledged her existence. I was envious of that, which was silly of me. I was also angry that she left. She promised we'd still spend time together. She even told me I could spend the summer with her, but she lied. She never did come back for me." If Dr.

Lewis couldn't lead me where I wanted to go, I'd get there on my own, dammit. I hadn't realized the truth until I'd said it, and I was surprised at the flood of emotions I felt reliving the memories. It still hurt.

"Good job, Lena," she said, as though she'd somehow contributed to my revelation and could now award me a gold star. "That's probably the most honest you've ever been with me."

"So where does that get me? I'm in jail on trial for murdering my family. I don't see forgiveness anywhere in my future."

"Whose forgiveness do you want?"

"Rebecca's."

"Do your future actions depend on Rebecca's forgiveness?"

That question actually required my attention. "What do you mean?"

"You're a smart lady. Think about it for a minute."

So she'd decided to show up for work, after all. *Do my future actions depend on Rebecca's forgiveness?*

I thought back, sorting through memories as if they were old photographs arranged in an album, some worn and ragged around the edges, others painfully sharp. Some of the memories were of Rebecca, snapshots of her dressing me, feeding me, parenting me. I was in those mental pictures with her, receiving what she had to give. I tried to explain my thoughts to Dr. Lewis.

"What were you feeling?"

Good question. A gold star for Dr. Lewis. What was I feeling? I felt anxious. I was afraid Rebecca would handle me too roughly, or that she'd lose her temper and snap at me. I was afraid she'd become impatient and leave me behind, and then what would I do? Who would help me? I was afraid my mother would walk in and say something hurtful. She had a way of doing that.

Rebecca, can you do anything with that rat's nest on your sister's head?

God, Lena, can't you stay clean for one minute? You're always so filthy.

I don't have time for this. I need to get Callie dressed. Rebecca, try to keep her out of my way.

I was afraid she'd give Rebecca something else to do, some other responsibility in order to lighten her own load, and Rebecca would take her frustrations out on me. When that happened, there was nowhere for me to go, no one to turn to. There was only Rebecca.

And I was afraid of Rebecca. I relied on her, because she was all I had.

I loved her, because she was the one who took care of me.

But I was afraid of her.

My stomach knotted with the memory. I opened my eyes to the blue sky, white clouds drifting lazily in the warm spring breeze. A row of sparrows sat at eye level on the powerlines stretched along the sidewalk in front of the building, while a fly crawled across the stained and scratched plastic table we bracketed, stopping partway to clean himself, legs busily rubbing together. I could hear traffic sounds on the street below and smell hot tar from the roofs around me, already heating up as the sun climbed overhead. Dr. Lewis sat across from me, quiet, observing. I felt safe. There I sat, on the roof of a jail, my own cell beneath my feet, potentially facing the death penalty. And I felt safe.

"Afraid," I finally answered Dr. Lewis' question.

"You didn't feel safe with Rebecca?"

"No, I didn't feel safe. I felt brittle, on edge, always mindful of her breaking point."

"Where does your father fit in? What are his snapshots?"

Memories of my father aren't as clear. They're blurry, as if my mental camera caught him in a moment of action. Yelling, gesturing, slamming doors, slapping me. What am I feeling? Fear, of course, but also anger. Rebecca and my mother had the power to hurt me. My father enraged me. I said as much to Dr. Lewis.

"Why do you think that is?"

"With them, Rebecca and my mother, there was always the possibility of acceptance. I always thought if I could just act right, not get in the way, not cause any trouble, they were within reach. When I felt rejected by them, it hurt. It was different with him. I'd never experienced anything *but* rejection from him. He was completely closed off to me." I paused to gather my thoughts. "Rebecca has a few good memories of time spent with my father, but I don't. She once accused my father of not wanting me, and I think she was right. That was the crux of everything, really. After Callie was born, with all the complications and everything, I don't think he wanted another child, and he was angry about it. About me. That's all he ever felt towards me, so it became what I felt towards him."

"Very insightful, Lena. Good job. Now that you've more clearly defined the dynamics of your family, your childhood, how can you use the information to help you move forward?"

Across the street, a car backed carefully into a space along the curb. A dark-haired young woman in a gauzy yellow sundress jumped out and opened the back door, bending over for a minute before emerging with an infant in her arms. I almost thought I could hear her talking, comforting the baby as she stepped onto the walk, cradling the child against her chest with one hand while feeding the meter with the other. I could have sworn I caught a strain of music, a soft soprano, the words to "Hush, Little Baby" floating up to the rooftop where I sat.

"I don't know, Dr. Lewis," I answered her. "I don't even know where *forward* is. But I do know I want something different."

"Back to my first question: Do your future actions depend on Rebecca's forgiveness?"

"No." I answered without hesitation. "I wish I could have it. I miss my sister, and I'm sorry for the way I've treated her. But even without her forgiveness, I want to do better. To be different. I just don't know what that looks like or how to get there."

"That's the first time I've ever heard you hint at a future."

"It is?"

"Our sessions are always about the past, about your anger. When I've tried to lead you to change, you've resisted. When I've asked what you want out of life, you've laughed at me. Until now, I've never heard you speak as if you believe you have some control over what happens to you, as if you might be able to shape your own outcome."

"I don't think I've ever believed I can. I'm still not sure I can, but I'd like to try. Being here has given me a lot of time to think. Not to *react*, but to think, without worrying about starving to death or freezing to death or someone having sex …" I stopped. It was time to be honest with myself. "Without having to worry about getting raped." I felt a piercing ache deep in my heart when I said the words. For the first time in years, tears welled in my eyes, so I looked away. "Can we sit here for a little while?" I asked, my voice choked. "Just sit without talking for a few minutes before you have to go?"

"Of course. Take all the time you need. While we sit, I have one more thing I'd like for you to think about."

"What's that?"

"You've talked about wanting Rebecca's forgiveness."

"So?"

"Do you forgive Rebecca?"

Across the street the young mother continued down the sidewalk, her dress floating behind her in the wind. She reached the corner and turned, disappearing from view. The sun was warm; it made me sleepy. I leaned my head back against the chair, closing my eyes and listening. *Hush little baby, don't you cry … Daddy loves you and so do I …*

Chapter 28: Brian Stone

I WAS LOCKING my office for the day when my cell rang. Wrestling it out of my pocket, I looked down to see Rebecca's number on the screen.

"What can I do for you?"

"Brian." Her voice was hesitant, and I could hear other voices in the background, quite a few of them. "We've had a new development."

"What's happened?" I cradled the phone between my neck and shoulder, balancing briefcase and lunch cooler in one hand while punching the elevator key with the other. "Is it Lena?"

"Lena's fine. At least I assume she is. But today was the first day of the auction."

"And? How'd it go?"

"Definitely not as planned," she said. "The police are here now."

"What's going on?"

"Remember I told you my parents had a lot of junk? Well, I had to divide the auction up into inside and outside. Today was outside. Farm equipment, mainly. It was going well. We'd sold nearly all of dad's hand and power tools, as well as the tiller and lawnmower. We'd gotten to the farm truck, not the truck we drove to town, but that old, rusted truck sitting out back. The Chevy half-ton? The auctioneer decided to give people five minutes to look it over before bidding started."

"And?" She was taking entirely too long and I was growing impatient, the tension ratcheting up a notch with each inflection of her voice.

"And someone looked under the seat, one of the men, and … Brian? A hat was under there. And it's … it's covered with dried blood. It's William's. Your Willie G. He always wore it when he was working for Daddy. It's a nasty old Tennessee ball cap that used to be white but is so filthy it no longer is. Now it's … oh, God, Brian it was stuck to floor—literally *stuck* to it—with blood." A shaky breath. "I'm sorry. It's just so … ah, God."

"Catch your breath, Rebecca, before you hyperventilate. Who's there with you?"

"The cops. Bill. Bill Frazier is here."

"Can you put him on the line?"

"I don't know. Hold on."

I waited what seemed an eternity, listening to the background noise filtering through Rebecca's phone. Then, "Bill Frazier here."

"Bill, it's Brian Stone."

"Rebecca told me. I assume she told you why we're here."

"She did. How long before we get any results back on either the hat or the blood?"

"I'll ask Gina to put a rush on it. She'll do what she can, but it could still be a few weeks."

"This could be our first real proof that Willie G. was at the crime scene."

"Could be, but I don't need to remind you we have to take it one step at a time. Remember, now, his prints are bound to be all over that truck. He's driven it before. It's Eugene's old farm truck. Eugene didn't take it out on the road anymore. Didn't even have it registered or insured. But Rebecca said he still used it for getting around the farm, hauling wood, that sort of thing. Hell, keys are still in it, although it's been sitting so long it doesn't start."

"Any blood inside the truck aside from on the hat? Prints in blood, smears, that sort of thing?"

"We're still working the scene, Brian. Not too much I can tell you right now."

"I understand. I'll have to request a continuance and keep my fingers crossed it's granted. I appreciate your hard work, Bill. How's Rebecca holding up?"

"About like you'd expect. A little shaken up."

"How about Lena? Has anyone let her know?"

"Not that I know of. We're pretty busy out here."

I consulted my watch. "I'll try to get in to see her this evening," I said. "Given the circumstances, I don't think that should be a problem."

"I appreciate that, Brian. It would be best if she heard it from either you or Rebecca, and I'm afraid Rebecca is going to be tied up here for a while."

"Is she planning on staying out there, even after this?"

"Says she is. Says she doesn't have anywhere else to go. Can't afford a hotel. I'd invite her to stay with me and the missus if I could, but that won't fly given my involvement in the investigation."

"I'll give her a call later tonight to check in. She can bunk with me, if she's willing. I have a huge guest room just sitting empty." It had been empty since the last time Phillip and Anna had visited, several years before.

"That's going above and beyond the call of duty, Brian, but that's why I sent them to you in the first place."

"From what I hear, I'm not the only one going above and beyond. Tell, me, Bill, who's been paying for Lena's therapy all these years? On second thought, don't answer that. I'm sure it's just gossip."

"I don't know what you're talking about."

"Keep denying it, and keep your methods murky. Otherwise you're looking at another potential conflict of interest."

"Nothing to worry about, Brian. Like I said, I don't know what you're talking about."

"You're a damn fine man, Bill."

"Not really," he said. "That little girl never stood a chance."

His words surprised me. He'd let his professional mask slip for a moment.

"It's a sad situation," I agreed.

"Someday soon I'll retire," he said. "Not soon enough, that's for damn sure. But soon. When that day comes, you should take me out for a beer."

"I'll definitely do that," I said. "I look forward to it, with bells on."

"Leave off the bells," he responded, "or the deal's off. I've seen enough weird shit during my career to last a lifetime."

We ended the call, and I stood for a moment in the parking garage, feeling the breeze from the Mississippi wash across my face. It was a clear night, warm but not humid, and I imagined I could smell the ancient scents of the river over the modern scents of asphalt and exhaust fumes, could feel the pull of the currents as they rushed through the night.

I'm not a man who believes in invisible higher powers. Having grown up the way I did, I'm a man who believes in the power of self. Study hard, work hard, and you can make something of yourself. You can overcome the sorry circumstances into which you were born and create a new life.

And yet, as I stood sniffing the wind and feeling the tremendous power of those dark, roiling waters, I had to admit something was at work. As a young adult I met Phillip, and then Anna, both of whom changed the trajectory of my life. There was a connection, a *recognition*, I can't describe. I loved them both immediately, but it was more than that. It was as if we were meant to meet. As if we were each a part of a larger design, one we couldn't see, but which was there, nonetheless.

I was experiencing that same phenomenon with Rebecca and Lena Reynolds. I had the distinct feeling they were meant to be in my life at this particular time. I didn't know for what purpose, but I knew when the case was concluded, I wouldn't be the same man I'd been when it began.

That was no doubt a good thing.

Chapter 29: Lena

I DIDN'T WANT to go to prison.

When I was first arrested, I didn't care. There were three reasons for this.

First, I couldn't believe I'd be found guilty of murdering my family, because I couldn't believe I'd done it.

Second, jail might not be the most pleasant environment, but in many ways, it was better than what I'd had. If you can get past the whole *imprisonment* part, it's not half bad. I'm talking about *jail*, mind you, which I realize isn't the same as prison. I'd heard as many horror stories as anyone else about the horrors of prison—rapes, beatings, and the like—but that didn't worry me, either. Hell, I'd dealt with those on the outside, just not with some of the benefits I'd get in prison.

Third, and maybe most significant, I believed I needed to be punished. Whether or not I had murdered my parents—and I wasn't convinced I had—I'd gotten away with enough bad things in my past I believed it was only fair I pay the price. Dr. Lewis once suggested I had a subconscious belief that I should be punished for the added burden my existence added to my already emotionally-stretched parents. At that time, I didn't know if I agreed with her; it was a lot to wrap one's mind around, and truthfully, I wasn't even sure it made sense. Either way, I'd lucked out of enough legitimate punishments I didn't feel I could complain about an undeserved one—assuming, as I did, it was undeserved.

But over time, as the months dragged on and I had time to think, I began to care. There were three reasons for this, as well.

First, I'm an idiot in more ways than you can count, but even I knew how damning the evidence was. Prison was no longer an abstract concept; it was damn near a reality, and the reality was a hell of a lot scarier than the abstract concept.

Second, I began to think maybe I didn't deserve to be punished, after all, at least not for something I didn't believe I'd done. Maybe Dr. Lewis' theory was correct, to some extent. Maybe I was born into a world in which my guilt was predetermined. If you can bear with me a moment, I'll try to explain this better than Dr. Lewis did.

My earliest memories are of feeling guilty. I felt guilty when I, a curious little girl, made a mess someone had to clean. I felt guilty when I needed help in the bathroom. I felt guilty when I was hungry and had to bother someone to feed me. I didn't always understand exactly what their words were, but I always understood the anger and exhaustion behind them, and I knew I was the cause of it. I was well aware I was a burden. I caused problems. In my mind, this made me *bad.* There was no way for me to fix it; I was simply bad.

The longer I sat in jail, the more I began to realize what a fucked-up way of thinking that was. I was just a baby, for heaven's sake. I didn't ask to be born. The more I turned it over in my mind, the more it seemed to me that *I* wasn't the problem; *they* were. They royally screwed me over from the day they took me home from the hospital.

That doesn't negate all the bad things I've done in my life, but it does give me a new way of looking at things. Maybe I wasn't born bad after all. Maybe I had some good in me. I'd believed I was bad, so I was bad. Maybe if I believed I was good, I could be good. I thought it was at least worth a shot.

That's a simple way of putting it, but it's the best I can do.

The third reason I began to care started with Teresa Johnson. I met Teresa in the dayroom. She was a tiny woman, maybe five feet tall if she stretched, ninety pounds soaking wet. She was sitting by herself in a chair in the corner, not even looking at the T.V. I sat near her, not because I wanted to, but because that seat happened to be close enough to the television to see it, but far enough away from Stacie Dodd, a known agitator who seemed to think she owned the room and everyone in it.

The Price is Right was on, an ancient one, and women were laughing and calling out answers that were hilariously wrong for the outdated show. I wasn't participating, other than to laugh at some of the more outlandish guesses. I wasn't afraid of Stacie Dodd, but neither did I want to earn her attention. I knew how to be invisible; I'd had a lot of practice.

I'd been sitting there a good ten minutes before the woman in the corner spoke. "Teresa Johnson," she said, holding out a hand. I was struck by her formality. The women of Block 1 slapped each other five, gave each other dap, or pretended not to see each other. What we *didn't* do was shake hands. Still, I found myself reaching back toward her, giving her hand a good shake. She had a surprisingly strong grip for such a small woman, her skin cold and dry.

"Lena," I said. I didn't offer my last name, and thankfully, she didn't ask. The last thing I needed was a jail full of inmates making the connection between me and my father.

"Today is my son's birthday," she said, settling back into her original position in the corner.

"That's nice," I said, unsure where she wanted to go with that. It wasn't the sort of conversation I usually had with my fellow inmates. "Will you get to speak to him?"

"Oh, no," she said. "I lost him a long time ago."

I wasn't sure what to say to that, either, so I gave her a vague nod and turned back to the T.V.

"They took him away," she said, sitting forward again. "Right after he was born. They've taken all my kids away."

She didn't say this with any apparent sadness, but as a statement of fact. I turned to look at her again. She was quite a bit older than I and didn't wear it well. She might once have been pretty, but there were no remnants left from that time. Her gray hair was thin and lank, her face worn and wrinkled. I could see swollen blackheads along the sides of her nose and across her forehead, and a whisker or two under her chin. I was struggling to come up with an appropriate response when she said, "You probably think I'm old."

"No," I said, pulling my gaze from her chin. "Not at all."

"How old do you think I am?"

"I'd guess sixty? Sixty-five?" I sought to be generous.

She laughed. "Fifty-eight," she said. "This is what hard living will do to you."

I hadn't considered myself to have had an easy life, but I knew I still looked decent for my age. I wondered what sort of life had aged her to such an extent.

"Bad choices," she said, as if reading my thoughts. "That's what did it."

"I know what that's like," I said, finally feeling as if I were on steady ground. "I've made a few of those myself."

"Why?" she asked.

"Why?" I repeated. "I don't know why." Who was this bitch to question me? "Why did you?" Across the room, I heard the unmistakable theme song for *The Love Boat*. What the hell channel did they have that T.V. on, anyway?

"Until now, I was too stupid to know any better," she said.

"And now you do?" Sure she did. Everyone in jail knows better. Until they get out of jail again, anyway.

"Oh, sure, now I do," she said, "but it's too late."

"Is that right?" I moved slightly away from her, not really caring about her answer, angling myself toward the T.V. again. I never did like *The Love Boat*, not even when it was exciting and new, as the song says.

But my conversation with Teresa Johnson was going nowhere and she was making me uncomfortable.

"I'm dying," she said. "Lung cancer. Too late to do anything about it." I noticed then the bluish skin around her mouth, the wheeze as she spoke. "You know the saddest thing?" She leaned forward again, in my line of vision. I shook my head, and she continued, rocking slightly and staring off into the distance. "Nobody gives a damn. Not one person. When I die, I'll be buried on your dime. Well, not yours, because you look to be on the same path I took, but with taxpayer money. A pauper's grave, they used to call it. Bulldozed over like garbage. That's the saddest part of the whole damn story."

"Is it really the saddest part?" I asked, and her head snapped around faster than I'd have thought she could move, her dark eyes staring into mine. I stared right back at her. "Somehow, I don't think so."

"I don't reckon I know what you mean."

I wasn't sure myself, exactly, but something about her self-pity struck me as wrong. "I guess I'd think having all my kids taken away was the saddest part," I answered.

She laughed, or at least I assumed it was a laugh. She emitted a loud, phlegmy bark before doubling over in a coughing fit. I sat and waited, torn between smacking her on the back—what good could it do at this point?—and simply waiting for her to finish. I opted for the latter, and after what seemed an impossibly long time she inhaled a raspy, hitching breath and sat back up, wiping her eyes.

"You're right about that, ain't you?" She was grinning, showing a mouth full of rotted teeth. "I'm a selfish old bitch. Never could seem to make myself do the right thing."

She stood up slowly, grasping my shoulder for support, then shuffled out of the dayroom without another word to me. I heard a few days later she'd been taken to the hospital, and a few days after that she had died.

I had no idea what was about to happen with me, but I knew I didn't want to be another Teresa Johnson. I didn't want to die old and wrecked and alone and be buried in a pauper's grave. It had started with Brian's anger toward Willy G., his outrage at the way I'd been treated even in the face of my denial, and his steadfast belief in my worth as a person when I believed I had none. After years of therapy, it took his belief in me for something to finally click. Dr. Lewis and I had been building on that shaky foundation a little at a time, and for the first time in my life I had hope for a better future. Hell, hope for any sort of future at all.

I didn't want to go to prison, and while I had my relationship with Lenny as an ace up my sleeve, that wasn't good enough. I wanted a jury to find me innocent of the murder of my family. I wanted to *be* innocent of the murder of my family. I didn't want to be the sort of person who could do something like that, and I didn't want a mistrial. I didn't want the prospect of a future trial hanging over my head. I wanted to walk out that door with my head held high enough to see my future life.

Chapter 30: Brian Stone
August, 2016

"WE GO BACK to court next week, and we have some things to think about." I set my briefcase on the table and took a seat across from Lena.

"Uh-oh. That doesn't sound good."

I looked at Lena, noticing, not for the first time, how different she was from the woman I'd met months before. Long gone were the sexually provocative gestures and angry rebuttals. Her hair had grown longer and was pulled back into a simple ponytail at the nape of her neck, her face make-up free. She was an attractive woman, simply and easily pretty in nothing more than her county-issued jumpsuit.

My first thought was that she more closely resembled Rebecca than I'd previously thought, but that wasn't quite true. Physically, yes, but I'd been surprised to realize Lena had a calmness about her that Rebecca didn't share. The rocking, shifting restlessness was nowhere to be seen. She sat quietly—serenely, even—

regarding me steadily as I loosened my tie and took off my jacket.

"Nothing bad," I said, "just something to discuss. A proposal upon which we must excogitate."

She laughed. "You and your big words."

"Excogitate," I repeated, enunciating each syllable. "It's a great word, isn't it? By the way, I must say you're looking well."

"Thank you. So are you, although you're in need of a haircut. Your curls are spiraling out of control." She smiled, and I returned the gesture with a feeling of warmth.

"I was thinking of going for more of a bohemian look," I said.

"To go with your move to the country?"

She said it teasingly, but she was closer to the truth than she could have known. I'd been looking at what could best be described as a cabin, not a trendy, cookie-cutter replica, but an honest-to-God cabin set on twenty acres of land south of President's Island, butted up against Mallard Lake. Hardwood timber, whitetail deer, wild turkeys, freshwater fishing … what more could a person want? It was perfectly located, a beautiful slice of country a mere twenty minutes from my downtown office.

Phillip and Anna would have loved it, and therein was my dilemma. They would have loved it, but they'd never see it, a thought that hurt my heart. I hadn't made an offer, though I had met—twice— with the realtor. I just needed to be sure. I needed to know my good memories of Phillip and Anna would replace my bad ones, and I wasn't sure I was there yet.

"I've made you sad," said Lena. "What did I say?"

"No." I hurried to reassure this woman, this newly empathic Lena. "Not sad, just thoughtful." I snapped open my briefcase to pull out my laptop. "On that note, let us think."

She laughed again, and I found myself enjoying the sound. She had a deep laugh. Husky, from the diaphragm. Until that moment, I hadn't known. Any laughter I'd heard previously had been tinged with bitterness. This laugh was pure.

"On anything in particular?" she asked. "Or is this more of a mental exercise to get the synapses firing again?"

"I do have something in particular, as it happens. They're offering a plea deal."

The smile disappeared. "A plea deal? So the charges won't be dropped, then."

"The charges won't be dropped," I confirmed, "but the prosecutor is willing to reduce them."

"To what?"

"Involuntary manslaughter. You'd be looking at three to fifteen years."

"Instead of life in prison."

"Or capital punishment. I don't mean to be harsh, but you need to understand the reality of the situation, Lena. Tennessee law allows capital punishment for crimes deemed particularly cruel or atrocious. Your family's murder, the way it was committed, certainly meets that definition. That's what they'll ask for."

"I know." She sighed. "I've known. So if I say I'm guilty and accept the deal, I'll be guaranteed no longer than fifteen years. If I take my chances at trial, I'll either be acquitted, or I'll be killed."

"That sums it up fairly well."

"What do you think, Brian? What should I do?"

The look of complete trust she gave me was almost frightening. "Why don't you sleep on it?" I suggested. "You don't have to make a decision tonight, and keep in mind we can negotiate."

"Meaning what? Ask for the minimum?"

"That's one possibility, among others."

Lena sat quietly for a moment, presumably lost in thought. I'd nearly decided it was time to excuse myself, but then she spoke. "This would be easier if I knew whether or not I'd done it. Then I'd know whether or not I deserve the punishment."

"You didn't do it, Lena. We have experts lined up to testify you couldn't possibly have done that and walked away unscathed, without a mark to show for it. You know this."

"I wish I knew what part I played."

"Willie G. took you there. As far as what part you played, your worst crime was in trusting that sorry bastard. He drugged you up and planted you at the crime scene, a damn near perfect plan, as I told your sister."

"My sister. How is she?"

"A little overwhelmed, I think, with trying to wrap everything up at the old house. She has her hands full. They didn't leave things in the best of shape, but then I don't suppose they knew they were leaving it at all."

"Nice try, Brian, but that isn't why she hasn't come to see me."

"No, probably not. You two have a lot of baggage between you."

"That's a nice way of putting it. On to lighter topics: so you think I should take the deal."

It was a statement, not a question. I hesitated before answering, well aware of the gravity of my responsibility in that moment.

"Brian?"

"We have a strong case," I said. "The tests have all come back, and there's room for reasonable doubt. They realize that, too. If they didn't they wouldn't have offered the deal."

She held my gaze for several long seconds. "You think we can win."

"There are no guarantees, Lena. I think we can win—I think we *should* win—but juries are unpredictable. And if we lose …"

"I trust you," she said, and my heart thudded in my chest. Trust was a terrifying proposition, I had learned, not only for the one trusting, but also for the one trusted. *Especially* for the one trusted, if my experience was anything to go by.

"All I can promise is I'll give it my all," I said. "I can't promise we'll win."

"Your all is good enough for me," she replied, stretching her cuffed arms across the table. I reached across, meeting her halfway and taking her hands in mine. I felt a nearly overwhelming urge to lift her hands to my cheek, not in an erotic way, but an affectionate way. A *familiar* way.

"I trust you," she said again.

"And I believe in you."

I saw tears gather in her eyes at the same moment I felt my own moisten. I released her hands and stood, the room suddenly too small to contain my emotions.

Fealty, I could hear Phillip whisper against my shoulder, the last word he'd ever spoken to me. *Prom-*

ises, grasped hands, declarations of trust and loyalty. It was too much. I'd been there before; I didn't want to go there again.

"Tomorrow, then," I said, my voice deceptively cheerful, echoing off the walls of the tiny room. I slammed my briefcase shut with more force than I'd intended and moved toward the door.

Lena looked at me, a brief look of what appeared to be concern flashing across her face before she stood and readied herself for the guard. "Tomorrow," she said, then paused. "Brian?"

"What?"

"Are you okay? You seem … I don't know what you seem. Something."

"I'm fine." I forced a smile. "We've got this."

She nodded. "I know we do. But if it doesn't work, I have an ace up my sleeve. I don't want to use it, but I will if I have to."

Like a splash of cold water, her admission brought me back to the present. The walls receded, and my vision cleared. "What do you mean? Lena, what are you talking about?"

She tilted her head toward the approaching guard. "Nothing we need to talk about right now. Just something to remember."

"If you know something—anything at all that could help us—you need to tell me."

"I will if I need to," she promised, "but it's better this way. If I can be acquitted, if I can walk out of here knowing this is all behind me and there's no chance of having to do it all again—if I can walk out of here knowing I'm innocent—that's the way I want to do it. I want to start over, Brian, with a clean slate."

That was a sentiment I could understand. I let her go without pressing the issue.

Chapter 31: Trial Transcript
August, 2016

Court Clerk: State your name for the record, please.

Dr. Grouse: Stephen Joseph Grouse.

The Court: Your witness, Mr. Stone.

Defense Attorney: Thank you, Your Honor. Dr. Grouse, tell the Court your credentials, please.

Dr. Grouse: I am the Crime Laboratory Director for L & M Diagnostics. Among various other duties, we do DNA testing and analysis for the Owensfield Police Department. I also teach graduate level forensic science and criminal justice courses at the University of Memphis. I obtained my Ph.D. from the University of Tennessee in 1979, and I'm certified by the American Board of Criminalistics, as well as by the International Association for Identification.

Defense Attorney: Thank you, Dr. Grouse. On the morning of June 8, 2016 you were contacted by Mrs. Gina McDivit of the Owensfield Police Department. Is that correct?

Dr. Grouse: That is correct. Mrs. McDivit spoke to me regarding several blood, hair, and fingerprint samples that needed testing. She asked me to put a rush on it, as the case had already gone to trial and a continuance would be needed until analysis was completed.

Defense Attorney: What samples, specifically, did she want you to test?

Dr. Grouse: Blood samples from five specific locations, including blood from a ball cap; blood from the driver's side floorboard of a 1991 Chevy half-ton; and blood from the steering wheel, driver's side door, and driver's side seat of that same vehicle. In addition, there were fifty-seven fingerprint samples taken from the vehicle, including thirty-five prints left in blood. Mrs. McDivit also needed DNA analysis performed on seven hairs, five taken from the ball cap, and two from the vehicle. The final specimen appeared to be a small sliver of bone, also retrieved from the driver's side floorboard.

Defense Attorney: Did you receive anything else from the Owensfield Police Department in relation to their submitted request?

Dr. Grouse: They also submitted standards from the victims.

Defense Attorney: Standards? Can you explain for those of us unfamiliar with the terminology?

Dr. Grouse: Certainly. The Owensfield Police Department also submitted blood and hair specimens from the victims in this case, as well as fingerprint samples.

Defense Attorney: Why would they do that, Dr. Grouse?

Dr. Grouse: Well, in a typical crime scene there may be mixtures of DNA on a specific item. For example, we might find the hair of one person mixed with the blood of another. With this particular crime scene and the number of victims, it's important for us to definitively identify all of the evidence. This is necessary in order to accurately reconstruct the crime scene.

Defense Attorney: Dr. Grouse, I'm now showing you what's been marked as Defendant's Exhibit D for Identification. Do you recognize this document?

Dr. Grouse: I do. That's the initial typed request submitted by Mrs. McDivit. It arrived later that morning, along with the samples.

Defense Attorney: Does this request truly and accurately describe the items submitted for testing and analysis?

Dr. Grouse: Yes, it does.

Defense Attorney: We would ask the Court to admit Defendant's Exhibit D as Defendant's #6.

The Court: Any objections?

Prosecutor: No, Your Honor.

The Court: Defendant's Exhibit D will be introduced into evidence as Defendant's #6.

Defense Attorney: Dr. Grouse, did you personally analyze the submitted samples?

Dr. Grouse: No. Unfortunately, these days my duties tend to be more administrative. It's a pity, because I miss that part of the work.

Defense Attorney: So you assigned them to your technicians?

Dr. Grouse: Yes. We had three different departments involved: one to analyze the blood and bone samples, one to analyze hair samples, and one to analyze fingerprints. I oversaw the three departments, and coordinated their findings into the final report submitted to the police department.

Defense Attorney: Dr. Grouse, I'm showing you what's been marked as Defendant's Exhibit E for Identification. Do you recognize this document?

Dr. Grouse: I do. That's the final report I submitted to the Owensfield Police Department.

Defense Attorney: We ask the Court to admit Defendant's Exhibit E for Identification as Defendant's #7.

The Court: Does the prosecutor have any objections?

Prosecutor: No, Your Honor.

The Court: Defendant's Exhibit E will be introduced into evidence as Defendant's #7. At this time we'll break an hour for lunch and reconvene at 1:00, at which time you can continue, Mr. Stone.

Chapter 32: Rebecca

THE TRIAL GROUND on, and the circumstances surrounding the deaths of my family members dominated my life longer than I'd ever thought possible. Every time it seemed Brian gained ground, the prosecutor did his best to tear testimony apart. I became convinced through the process that truth was nowhere in the equation. Both sides simply wanted to win. I suppose that was a good thing for us, but it didn't do much to enhance my faith in the criminal justice system.

When I wasn't in court, I continued to empty the house and grounds of my parents' possessions. Anything of true value had sold at the auctions, but boxes and bins and drawers and closets full of junk remained. As soon as there was space available, I'd moved the furniture from my previous apartment out of my father's shed and into the living room—the breeziest room in the house due to windows on two walls—and that was where I lived, as if it were a tiny, un-air-conditioned studio apartment.

The first time Brian saw my setup, he gave me an odd look. Initially, I didn't understand, but then he glanced at the floor, over in front of the door, and I knew. I'd hired cleaners immediately after being granted access back into the house, but there were still stains on the hardwood floors, if one knew where to look.

"Doesn't it bother you?" he asked. "You can stay at my place, you know. No strings attached. I'm talking a purely platonic arrangement. This isn't some sort of ploy to … well, you know. I just … I mean, my God, Rebecca …"

"I'm fine," I said, brushing away his concerns. "Truthfully, I don't even think about it. That was one moment in time—a terrible moment, I'll grant you, but still a moment. That's not what I see when I sit in this room."

That was true. Neither did I see the ghosts of happy family gatherings: game nights at the coffee table; the transparent, other-worldly figures of my family sharing a bowl of popcorn during movie nights; the apparition of my mother passing around mashed potatoes at family dinners full of laughter and conversation. I didn't see *those* things because they'd never happened, but I didn't feel the need to explain more to Brian.

It was odd, taking load upon load of my parents' possessions to the dump. I knew I should have felt something, some degree of melancholy, a pensive sadness as I sorted through the mouse-eaten detritus of my childhood—of my *family*—but I didn't. I felt no emotional connection whatsoever as I bent and lifted, heaved and shoved. I only felt a small sense of satisfaction at making a dent in the garbage.

I've said it before, and I'll say it again: I didn't hate my parents. I didn't harbor anger. Certainly not to the extent Lena had. What I felt on those long, hot nights as I worked my way through their closets was … *nothing*. I felt nothing at all.

Occasionally, when I came across something of Callie's, I felt what can best be described as a faint wisp of regret—for her. Not for me. I wonder sometimes what Callie's life could have been like had my mother's doctor not been trolling for whores down in the bottoms on the night she was born. What might it have been like if she'd been born into a different family, even with her disabilities intact? A family with enough love and joy to happily encompass a new member, even if that member came with an unusual résumé of challenges?

Those thoughts churned in my head during the long hours of solitude, as I sorted and bagged and attempted to force organization upon the chaos. What if Callie hadn't been born into a family in which she was used as a coat of armor? Because that's what she was, really. My mother had needed a reason to give in to her darker impulses, to withdraw from the world and stew in her own discontent. Callie was the perfect excuse.

I wondered how Callie had felt about that. Had she felt anything? Had she entertained thoughts she was unable to share? Did she understand enough about the world around her to realize the hopelessness of her situation? Were there ever times Callie sat in her wheelchair quietly rocking back and forth as she listened to my mother complain about the rising cost of Callie's meds; or the hardness of her stool; or the cluelessness of Callie's school aid; or her own, never-ending exhaustion, when Callie thought, "For God's sake, lady. Just shut the fuck up, already."

I sort of hoped there were.

I'd be listing the house soon. The farm. All of it. It had finally been decided I had that right. I was the executor, after all. Still, Lena had to sign paperwork before the decision was final. I had initially asked Brian to take it to her, but he'd refused.

"You take it," he'd said. "Rebecca. She's your sister. You really should go to see her."

"*You* should do it," I countered. "After all, damn near half the money from the sale is going to you, anyway."

He'd smiled at that, but he hadn't budged from his decision.

So I did as he'd suggested, the first time I'd been to see her since the trial had started. I'd noticed a change in her demeanor during the long days in court, but even so, I was taken aback by this new and improved Lena, the one I'd always wished for but never had. No bawdy jokes, no inappropriate comments. No anger. That was the biggest surprise. For the first time in nearly thirty years, Lena wasn't angry. I wasn't sure what to make of it. I didn't mention it to her, of course—what could I have said? "Gosh, Lena, it's nice to see you have a non-bitchy side"—but her newfound peace engendered a calmness in me, as well, taking the wind right out of my sails. So much so that when she apologized for the ways she'd hurt me over the years, I actually listened.

"I was angry," she said. "At you, at them. At everything. That's no excuse; I know that now. And I don't expect you to forgive me. I just want you to know I'm sorry."

I didn't tell her I forgave her, because I needed time to process the things she'd said. If at some point I offered forgiveness, I wanted to be sure it was real, not simply an emotional reaction to an emotional discussion. What I did offer her was an apology of my own.

"I'm sorry, too, Lena. I knew, even as I made promises, I wouldn't come back unless I had to. I couldn't say that to you, not back then. I knew it hurt you when I left, and I wanted to soften the blow as much as I could. I didn't stop to think about how you'd feel once you realized my promises had been empty." It was the truth. I *hadn't* stopped to think about how Lena would later feel—I was too intent on leaving—and I *was* sorry.

That was all we'd said about our acrimonious history that day. Really, what else was there? I had no idea what our relationship would look like moving forward, or if we'd have any sort of relationship at all. There was so much history, so much animosity, I wasn't sure we could move past it. I wasn't even sure I wanted to. At the end of the day, maybe the best either of us could hope for was a cessation of anger. That alone would be a relief. She'd signed the papers I'd offered and I'd thanked her and left. Aside from court, we hadn't seen each other since.

I wondered, as I left the courtroom after the judge's well-timed lunch dismissal the day of Dr. Grouse's testimony, if Lena would be able to maintain her calm once he began describing the findings in those reports. As for me, I had no intention of returning to court to sit and listen to a stranger categorize the bodily fluids and parts of my family members. It'd been hard enough to sit through the coroner's reports. I wouldn't put myself through that again.

Besides, I already knew. Brian had told me the findings. Blood, hair and various tissues from all three were found on the hat, floorboard, and seat. Fingerprints from my father, me, and Willie G. were found on the steering wheel and door handles, which wasn't surprising, since we'd all three driven the truck around the farm at various times. DNA from Willie G. was collected from a stain on the seat, "As if he'd lost control of his bladder," Brian had said. Given Willie G.'s persistent stench, that also wasn't surprising.

I hoped Brian had also warned Lena of what was to come. Unfortunately, she wouldn't have the luxury of skipping out, and I pitied her for that.

Chapter 33: Brian

IT WAS A miserably hot, sticky Sunday afternoon, and I was on my way to Owensfield. I'd gotten a call from Rebecca around 1:30 telling me some new information had come to light. It seems Rebecca had had a visitor, a Mr. Zebulon Pike, husband of Barbara Pike, owner of Barb's Country Cooking.

"They were friends of my parents," Rebecca explained. "Or at least what passed for friends. My parents didn't go out and socialize, but the Pikes went to the same church and had similar backgrounds."

"What did he want?" I'd asked, trying to move Rebecca along. She had a tendency, I'd learned, to get caught up in the details of a story and lose the point. As a friend—which I hoped to one day be—I was interested in the details, but as an attorney, I needed her to get to the point.

"He said he'd remembered something he thought might be helpful. He said he hadn't recognized Patty Sue, but when you made the connection between Patty Sue and Willie G. in court, he remembered something."

"Which was?" I'd been taking a rare day off, lounging at the pool for perhaps the first time ever. Before everything happened with Phillip and Anna I'd been too busy to take advantage of the amenities provided by my condo association. After their deaths I'd been too devastated. With the real possibility of moving out soon, I'd decided it was time to get my money's worth, but I'd no sooner slathered on sunscreen than my phone had rung. I'd nearly dropped it, struggling to answer it with lubed-up fingers.

"Which was my father talking to him about a handyman who'd been stealing from him."

"Shit!" At those words, I nearly dropped the phone again, but managed to catch it while hopping across the hot tiles on my way to dress and speed out to Owensfield.

We'd agreed to meet at the restaurant, Barb's Country Cooking. It was too late for lunch and too early for dinner, but Rebecca and I both agreed the house, without air conditioning, would be too miserable to hold any sort of extended meeting with Mr. Pike. The restaurant was about what I'd expected, older and a bit shabby, with the smell of hot grease permeating everything, but the iced tea was delicious and the dining area was cool and quiet. Mrs. Pike, a seemingly pleasant older woman, brought an extra pitcher of ice and left us to our business.

Mr. Pike was also about what I expected: a hard man. I don't know why I'd had that picture of him. Maybe it was because Rebecca had referred to him as her father's friend, and that's the way I'd come to think of Eugene Reynolds. Whatever the reason, my expectations had been met. He was tall and thin, still dressed in his black Sunday suit, thin, steely gray hair combed back from his forehead. Although he did manage to shake my hand, the dour expression he wore while doing so suggested I left a lot to be desired. "I don't much care for attorneys," he said by way of greeting.

"Neither do I," I said, both as an attempt to break the ice, and because it was largely true. If I'd expected a laugh, or even a smile, I was out of luck. Fine, then. Straight to business. "What is it you have to tell me?" I asked as we scooted our way into a booth, Mr. Pike and Rebecca on one side, me on the other.

"Eugene had a handyman he fired," he answered, struggling to remove his coat and lay it across the back of the booth behind him. He unbuttoned his cuffs, rolling them up in quick, jerky motions. "Man was stealing from him."

"Do you know it was William Wells?"

"Never had any other handyman I know about."

"Rebecca?"

She shook her head. "No. That was a point of contention between me and my father. I asked him repeatedly to hire someone to help with yardwork. It's a huge yard; you've seen it. It was too much for me to handle alone. But he refused. Truthfully, I doubt he was thinking of helping me when he hired Willie G. I think ..." She glanced at Mr. Pike. "I'm sorry, Mr. Pike. I know you and my father had a lot of respect for each other. I don't mean to speak ill of him, but as you probably know, we didn't always see eye-to-eye on things."

"None of my business," said Mr. Pike. "Eugene kept his family matters to himself, the way a man should."

Rebecca shot me a look I couldn't quite read, but continued. "Daddy would do things sometimes, things that seemed out of character given how tough he could be with us. Like, he'd pull off to the side of the road to hand a homeless man money, or spend hours volunteering somewhere, like the soup kitchen or the food pantry. When he did things like that, I always felt it was more for appearances than it was out of the kindness of his heart. My father was ever and always the politician." She looked sideways at Mr. Pike, but he continued to stare straight ahead, as if she hadn't spoken. "The short answer to your question is no, there were no other handymen. The long answer, as I'm sure you can see, is more complicated, but irrelevant to this conversation, I suppose."

"To this conversation, maybe, but not irrelevant," I said, and she gave me another look, different from the first, but no easier to identify. I turned back to Mr. Pike. "When was this? Do you remember?"

"It started back in the late spring, early summer before they were killed. He first noticed some small tools were disappearing. Nothing big. A screwdriver, one week, pair of pliers the next. Things a man might need for his own home, but not want to buy if it's right there for the taking and the man has a criminal bent. Eugene didn't have much patience for a man stealing. Neither do I. I told him right then and there he needed to get rid of the man."

"How did he respond?"

"Said he needed to make sure it was the handyman before doing anything."

"Who else could it have been?"

This time it was Mr. Pike who gave me an indecipherable look. Beside him, Rebecca stiffened.

"Your daddy wasn't accusing you, Rebecca. You need to understand that. But you were the only other person who had access to his tools, and before he fired a man, he needed to know it wasn't you. Borrowing them, but just without asking first. You understand?"

"I do," said Rebecca. "I certainly do." She slid out of the booth and stood. "I don't believe you gentlemen need me in order to finish your conversation."

"Rebecca—" I began, but she interrupted me.

"I'm not going to sit here and listen to this," she said. "I listened to it enough while he was alive."

"Wait for me, okay? We won't take long."

She nodded before turning and stalking towards the door, the tiny bells jingling a deceptively merry tune as she shoved it open.

"Was that really necessary?"

"I'm just telling the truth," said Mr. Pike. "Isn't that what you wanted?"

"What did Eugene Reynolds ultimately decide? Was Rebecca the one swiping his tools?"

"He caught the handyman red-handed. Man was trying to siphon gas from a five gallon can into his own tank."

"What did Mr. Reynolds do?"

"Fired him on the spot, is what he told me."

"You realize you'll have to testify."

"I do. Don't want to, but I'd like to see justice for Eugene, and his wife, too. Even for that little old crippled gal. I don't reckon life was worth much to her, but she deserves justice, too."

I stood and threw enough bills on the table to pay for the tea with a hefty tip left over. I had what I needed, and I had no desire to listen to him further.

Old is no excuse for ignorant. "You'll be hearing from me," I said, before hurrying outside to catch up with Rebecca.

She was pacing, walking circles around her car, clearly agitated.

"Let's go somewhere," I said. "Somewhere cool and quiet."

She shook her head. "I wouldn't be good company, Brian. I'm just … I can't get away from it." Her voice broke, and she covered her face.

"What did you have planned today?" I asked. "Before you were interrupted by all this."

"Not much, actually. I had a book I planned to read. I'd thought I'd go out under the elm where I might catch a breeze."

"Let's go do that," I said. "I'll follow you there. Unless, of course, you don't want my company."

She didn't answer, just stood quietly with her hands over her face until I moved toward her and enfolded her in my arms. To my surprise, she relaxed against me, sniffling into my chest. "I'm sorry, Brian. I'm just so tired of it all. It never ends."

"I know," I said, although I didn't really. I *wanted* to know, and hoped that counted for something. I stroked her hair, brushing it back from her face. Strands clung to her cheeks from a mixture of sweat and tears. Across the parking lot, Mr. Pike stopped and stared, then shook his head in apparent disgust— it was hard to get an exact read on his expression, since disgust seemed the default position—before lowering himself into a black 2015 Cadillac CTS and creeping out onto the highway.

Half an hour later we sat in lawn chairs under an old elm tree, sipping beers.

"You came prepared," Rebecca had said when she saw me making my way through the field to join her. I had indeed come prepared. I'd made a stop by the local Walmart and picked up a six-pack, a Styrofoam cooler, and a bag of ice. On my way through the checkout, I grabbed a pack of tissues just in case.

"Always," I said, smiling as I took a seat in the chair next to her and handed her a cold one. "I hope you don't mind the brand."

"Does it have alcohol?" she responded. "If it does, the brand is fine." Judging by the huge swig she took, it was more than fine.

"It's nice out here," I said, gesturing toward the field. "Must be ten, fifteen degrees cooler under this tree."

"It's the coolest place on the farm these days," she agreed, "but check yourself for ticks when you get home."

I wasn't sure if she was serious, but I made a mental note to examine myself as soon as I stepped foot back into the condo.

"Sorry about all that," she was saying. "I overreacted. He didn't say anything bad, really. I'm a little thin-skinned when it comes to my father's criticism, and that felt like more of it."

"I honestly don't think he meant anything by it, but it's hard to tell with him, isn't it? He's such a dour old man."

"For no good reason," said Rebecca. "They're one of the wealthiest families in town."

"So was yours," I reminded her, "and I wouldn't classify you or Lena either one as particularly happy."

"Touché," she said, touching her bottle to mine with a soft *clink*. "So is this your smoking gun? That he was fired shortly before my family was murdered?"

"I wouldn't call it a smoking gun, but it will certainly help build the case. Did you know your father had fired him shortly before the murders?"

Rebecca shook her head. "I didn't. He was there that Saturday morning, the one before they were killed. We'd both been tasked with repairing the fence along the north side of the property. All the rain had loosened some posts. We started on opposite ends and met in the middle, so we didn't talk much. I didn't see him after that."

"What time did you leave?"

"Later than usual, around six, after I cleaned the dinner dishes. I got home around ten, I remember, because I showered and went straight to bed. I work the day shift during the week, seven until three, so I'm usually in bed by ten, even on weekends. Otherwise my sleep schedule gets out of whack."

"Was he there when you left?"

"If he was, he was back in the field somewhere. I didn't see him."

"Did you see his car?"

She scrunched her forehead, as if trying to remember. "I don't recall seeing it, but I can't say for certain I would have noticed." She leaned toward me and sniffed. "You smell fruity," she said, and I felt myself blush.

"It's sunscreen."

"Pretty boy."

"I was at the pool ..."

"Working on your golden tan, getting those highlights in your curls the right shade of blonde?"

"You're as bad as your sister."

"Now *that's* something no one has ever said to me before." I couldn't see her eyes behind dark sunglasses, but her lips twitched, almost as if she were about to smile.

We sat in silence for a while, she with her head leaned back against the chair, and me taking in the scenery. It was a beautiful farm, gently rolling with cotton, the white bolls bright against the summer sky.

"Picking won't start for a few weeks," she said, startling me. "Sometime late September."

"I hadn't even thought about the farming aspect of your farm until now," I admitted. "I assume it's the same family that rented from your father?"

"It is." Rebecca sat up and reached for the cooler, rummaging around for two more beers, twisting off the tops before handing me one. "They're going to buy it."

"I hadn't realized you'd gotten that far," I said.

"You haven't been inside lately, have you?" she asked. "I'm nearly finished. Everything cleaned out. I'll hire a crew to come in and scrub it all down sometime this week."

"What in the world did you do with everything?" I asked. The last time I'd been inside Rebecca had moved all of her belongings into the living room as she sorted and disposed of boxes and bags from what seemed to be every conceivable nook and cranny. If I hadn't seen it with my own eyes, I'd never have believed so much junk could fit into such a modestly-sized house.

"The dump, most of it."

"Was there nothing you wanted to keep?"

"Nope. What would I do with old magazines and newspapers? What would *anyone* do with that? This house was a fire waiting to happen."

"Was there nothing of value?"

"Not after the auctions ended."

"Mementos? Family heirlooms?"

"Nothing. No school photos or old report cards. No macaroni art made in kindergarten or Christmas ornaments made from homemade dough. No locks of hair or baby teeth. Thank God for that, actually. I always thought hoarding hair and teeth was rather creepy."

"I'm with you on that."

She smiled again. "My mother wasn't the sentimental type. There was nothing to indicate anyone other than the three of them had ever lived here. Lots of diapers and medical supplies. Boxes of old dress patterns and yarns. Canning jars. Enough tools to fill Home Depot, with plenty left over for Ace Hardware."

"I'm sorry, Rebecca."

She tossed her hair back and wiped beads of sweat from her lip with the neck of her t-shirt. "It's okay. You grew up in foster homes, didn't you? So you probably don't have any of that stuff, either."

She was right; I didn't.

"Does it bother you?" she asked.

"No," I answered honestly. "It did at one time, but not now. I don't think I'd want anything stuffed in an attic or a storage locker that could remind me of that time in my life. I'm so far removed from it all now. I don't want anything tethering me to it, if that makes sense."

"Then you understand," she said. "There's no sadness connected to any of this. Even sitting here, under this tree. One of the few good memories I have is of sitting under this tree, but at the same time, one of the worst memories I have is of sitting under this tree. Nothing is untouched, *unsullied*, if you will."

"Unsullied," I smiled. "Good word."

She reached over and lightly punched me in the arm.

"Where will you go now?" I asked. "Back to your old apartment?"

"No. I let it go. I had to. There's nothing for me there, anyway. I'll still be here until the trial is over. We've agreed we won't sign the paperwork until the jury has reached a verdict. But then, when everything is squared away, I'll leave."

Something in her voice made me regard her more closely. "Leave to where?" I asked.

"I don't know. A road trip, maybe. I'll get enough out of the sale to last a while."

"What about Lena?"

"What about her? She'll have a little bit, too, after all your fees are paid. I've needed to talk to you about that. You'll have to arrange somehow for her to get it, if she gets out."

"*When* she gets out. And that's fine; I can do that. But that's not what I meant. I meant, what about your relationship with your sister? Are you going to tell her you're leaving? Let her know where you are?"

"Look, Brian, I know you've wanted us to sort things out, but there's really nothing to sort. Lena is Lena. She always will be, whether she's in prison or back down in the bottoms."

"Don't you care for her at all?"

"No," she said. "I know that shocks you. I'm sorry for that, for leaving you with the idea I'm a bad person. Maybe I *am* a bad person; I don't really know anymore. But I bet if you asked Lena, she'd say the same thing. At one time we may have shared a bond, but it was eroded a long time ago. I think we made peace with each other, if that makes you feel better."

"It's not me I'm worried about."

"Then it must be Lena, because there's no reason to worry about me. For the first time in my life, I'm almost free."

"Is that what you want?"

She smiled for the first time all day, a beautiful smile that lit up her face, erasing any trace of her earlier tears. "It is," she said. "It really, truly is."

Chapter 34: Trial Transcript

Court Clerk: State your name for the record, please.

Zebulon Pike: Zebulon Pike, named after the explorer.

Court Clerk: Spell your first name, please.

Zebulon Pike: Z-e-b-u-l-o-n.

Court Clerk: Thank you.

The Court: Your witness, Mr. Stone.

Defense Attorney: Thank you, Your Honor. Good morning, Mr. Pike.

Zebulon Pike: If you say so, Mr. Stone.

Defense Attorney: Did you make a phone call to Ms. Rebecca Reynolds the afternoon of August 21, 2016?

Zebulon Pike: I did.

Defense Attorney: And what was the purpose of that call?

Zebulon Pike: I remembered something I thought might be important.

Defense Attorney: What was it you remembered, Mr. Pike?

Zebulon Pike: I remembered a couple of conversations I had with Eugene Reynolds before he died.

Defense Attorney: When did you have these conversations?

Zebulon Pike: First was in the spring, a few weeks before he was killed. Sometime in early June, on a Sunday. We were talking after Sunday school while we were waiting for the preacher to get started with the sermon. I know it was early June because we were talking about the crops. The cotton was in, but we'd been having thunderstorms, fierce ones, you might remember, and we were commiserating on the possibility some of it might get washed away, and it was getting too late in the season to be replanting.

Defense Attorney: On this Sunday morning in early June of 2015, did Mr. Reynolds share information with you about a handyman he had hired?

Zebulon Pike: He did. He said he suspected the man had been stealing from him.

Defense Attorney: Did he tell you the handyman's name?

Zebulon Pike: If he did, I don't remember it. But Eugene only had one handyman I know of, the one he met up at the food bank. Man whose wife used to make fried apple pies from the apples on Eugene's farm.

Defense Attorney: And you say Mr. Reynolds suspected this man of stealing?

Zebulon Pike: Small things, he said. Like hand tools. A screwdriver, pair of pliers, that sort of thing.

Defense Attorney: What did Mr. Reynolds plan to do about it, if anything?

Zebulon Pike: Said he needed to make sure it was the handyman and not one of his daughters. He thought she might have been borrowing things and just forgot to tell him. Said if he found out the man was stealing from him, he was going to run him off the property.

Defense Attorney: By "run him off the property," did he mean fire him?

Prosecutor: Objection. Calls for speculation. Defense is asking the witness to read minds.

The Court: Sustained. Rephrase your question, Mr. Stone.

Defense Attorney: Did Mr. Reynolds clarify what he meant by saying he would "run him off the property?"

Zebulon Pike: Said he'd fire him and get a restraining order if the man set foot on Eugene's land again. Eugene wasn't partial to thieves.

Defense Attorney: Was that the last conversation you had with Mr. Reynolds regarding the handyman?

Zebulon Pike: No, it wasn't. We had another conversation a few weeks later, first part of July. Second week, if I have my times right. We were finally drying out. Lot of plants had washed out, but wasn't anything we could do about it by then.

Defense Attorney: Was this conversation also on a Sunday?

Zebulon Pike: It was. Same as before, waiting on the preacher to start preaching.

Defense Attorney: And Mr. Reynolds again mentioned his handyman?

Zebulon Pike: Sure did. Said he'd caught the man stealing gas the day before, siphoning from a gas can into his own tank.

Defense Attorney: What did Mr. Reynolds do?

Zebulon Pike: Fired him, just like he said he would.

Defense Attorney: Did the handyman leave?

Zebulon Pike: Eugene said he looked scared to death to have been caught. Tried to lie about what he was doing, but not much way to lie when you're caught sucking gasoline out of a can. Eugene told him he didn't have time to listen to his nonsense and he needed to just pack up and go. Said he stood and watched the man while he got in his car and drove away.

Defense Attorney: Did Mr. Reynolds hear from him again?

Zebulon Pike: Don't know. Next thing I heard, Eugene was dead.

Defense Attorney: Thank you, Mr. Pike. No further questions, Your Honor.

Chapter 35: Lena

"YOUR HONOR, the defense rests."

It was the last Friday in August, a hot, humid day that got even hotter when a light afternoon shower turned the air into steam. There was no rebuttal, thank God. I didn't think I could sit through more. Summations were all that were left, and they wouldn't take place until the following week. Until then, I had a long weekend ahead of me, with ample time to stew in my thoughts.

"Try not to worry too much."

Thankfully Brian had accompanied me back to the jail, and we now sat in our familiar seats across the table from one another. "You're asking the impossible," I told him. "Switch places with me, and you'll see."

"No way," he responded. "It sucks where you are."

As so often happened lately his response made me laugh, lifting the burden, if only for a moment. "How's Rebecca?" I asked. I'd wondered about her since our visit.

"I think she's okay." He hesitated. "Have you talked to her at all?"

"Not since she had me sign paperwork to sell the house."

"You have some from that, too, you know. Actually I have it, ready to give it to you when you're out."

I smiled. "I like the 'when' in your sentence."

"I thought you might."

"You haven't really answered me, though."

"About what?"

"Rebecca."

"I told you, I think she's okay."

"And then you hesitated and changed the subject."

"I did, didn't I? I hoped she would have contacted you."

"She hasn't."

"She's leaving after the trial. She said she's going to take a road trip."

"On a one-way street, no doubt," I said. Rebecca had been trying to escape as long as I could remember. Now was her chance.

"She should have told you."

"It's okay. Did she tell you we made peace? At least to the extent we can."

"She did."

"That's all that matters, really."

"That just seems so wasteful to me. I mean, you're sisters, for God's sake. Do you know what I would have given to have a sister? Or a brother? Or *anyone?*"

"But that's you, Brian, and those were different circumstances. We shared parents, but we weren't sisters.

Not really. She was a mother figure to me, and I was an aggravation to her. In a different time and place we might have been close, but we were never given that opportunity. We're too old and set in our ways to try to fake it now. But enough about that. What will you say about me?"

"When?"

"In your summation, of course. I already know what Mr. McDonald will say. He'll say I'm a sociopath. A whore who turns tricks for drugs. A heartless monster who murdered her family in cold blood after years of conflict. But what will you say? Stop looking so uncomfortable and lay it out there."

"I'll say you've made a lot of mistakes in your life. I'll say you prostituted yourself for drugs after you were kicked out of your house at the tender age of sixteen. You did what you had to do to survive, and yes, you've had your share of arrests. But none of them, ever, were for violent crimes."

"But I tried to murder—"

"But you didn't. Besides, that was self-defense. The only victim of your crimes was you. You did not murder your family; it's not physically possible. You were there, but against your will or even knowledge. You'd had the bad luck to fall in with a bad man who used you to get to your parents. He drugged you, dragged you in the house to get your prints on the wall, and dumped you back in the bottoms. The evidence shows this to be true, and he had the motive. The investigator testified the murders appeared to be a crime of passion based on the viciousness of the attack. That fits. Your father fired Willie G. and took away a source of badly needed income. Your father kept money at the house, and Willie G. knew where to find it. He also knew you'd been disowned, and he knew where to find you. Who better to pin it on?"

I thought over what he'd said. "Do you really believe that's what happened?"

"You did not kill your family, Lena. I believe that with all my heart."

"Will your summation work?"

"I think so. Yes."

"And if it doesn't?"

"You know what happens if it doesn't."

I did indeed. The way I saw it, I was faced with three possibilities. Acquittal was the first, and I was trusting Brian to make it happen. He seemed convinced we'd made a good case for reasonable doubt, and if there was a chance I'd be acquitted, I wanted to take that chance.

The second possibility was to be found guilty, but successfully throw Lenny under the bus. I didn't understand how everything worked, but I'd tell Brian about Lenny and he'd do whatever it is lawyers do to get the conviction overturned. From everything I'd heard it could take years, perhaps the rest of my lifetime, before anything happened, but it was at least a shot at freedom. A part of me still didn't want to betray Lenny, but another part knew what he was doing was wrong, even if in some twisted way it momentarily helped the people in the bottoms.

The third possibility was to be found guilty and denied an appeal. In that case, I'd be put to death.

"Have you thought about what you'll do when you get out?" Brian was asking.

"I haven't," I answered. "I've been too busy thinking about what happens if I don't."

"Well," he said. "The cabin comes with a spare room. No strings attached."

Chapter 36: Rebecca

I HAD TOLD Brian I would stay until I knew what was going to happen with Lena, and I kept my promise.

The jury had been deliberating for three days by the time I got the call. Just the evening before, a Thursday, Brian had bemoaned the possibility of a hung jury. "God, Rebecca," he'd said, his voice fading in and out with the terrible phone connection. "I hope we don't have to do all this again."

"I won't," I said, the words escaping before I could clamp my teeth together and keep them in.

"What do you mean, you won't?" he asked, as a new wave of static assaulted my ear.

"This is a terrible connection, Brian. I'm outside under the elm. Reception out here is awful, but it's too miserable for me to be anywhere else. I'll call you tomorrow." I clicked the phone off and dropped it onto the ground beside me before leaning my head back, eyes closed, grateful for the sudden quiet. I'd told Brian the truth; if we ended up with a hung jury, I wouldn't return for another trial. I had put my life on hold long enough. It was time to move on. Besides, I had little choice about the matter. In anticipation of a verdict, not realizing it would take the jury so long to decide, I'd signed the final paperwork just that morning, essentially selling myself out of a place to live, at least in the long-term.

"Stay as long as you need to." Mrs. Myers had waited for me in the lobby of the realtor's office after the paperwork was completed. She nodded toward her husband, who had pushed through the door and was striding across the parking lot with a vigor that belied his age. "You'll have to excuse him rushing off. He's not meaning to be rude, he's just anxious to get going. He absolutely hates taking time away from the fields, especially this time of year. But he's fine with you staying out at the house as long as you need to. He'll be by next week sometime to defoliate, but he shouldn't be in your way. Our plan is to eventually divide it up between the boys, if they ever settle down and get married. They don't know that, of course, but we thought it would give them a nice start. Plus, it'll keep them close so I can play with whatever grandbabies they end up giving me."

She laughed, and I wanted to say something friendly and polite, something along the lines of it being a wonderful place to raise a family, but an unexpected wave of grief washed over me, and I couldn't force the words around the lump in my throat. It *could* have been a wonderful place to raise a family. It *should* have been. But it wasn't.

"I appreciate the offer," I finally managed to say, and Mrs. Myers reached over and gave my arm a squeeze, no doubt thinking my sudden show of emotion was connected to leaving the old place, never imagining it was the staying that hurt me, not the leaving. With the exception of one lone suit hanging in the closet of the room I'd shared with Lena, my clothes were already packed, my toiletry bag on the bathroom vanity waiting to be filled. The house had been cleared of everything except my sleeping bag on the living room floor. I was living minute by minute, waiting for the jury to reach a verdict so I could move on with my life.

"Take your time," she said. "Give Lena our love. We think about her, Rich and me. We think about both of you. It's awful what happened, just terrible, a tragedy all the way around, but we've always loved you girls, and we still do, regardless." I'd thanked her a final time, eager to escape her incessant chatter. I waved to Mr. Myers, who leaned against their truck pointedly staring at his watch, and climbed into my car with a sigh of relief.

I'd stayed outside under the elm tree late into the evening, until mosquitoes forced me in, where I spent a restless night, the thick batting of my sleeping bag doing little to cushion the hard oak of the floor, the heat unrelenting. I'd finally given up just before dawn, taking a long, cold shower in an attempt to cool off.

So it was that I was up and bathed when I received Brian's early morning call. I nearly didn't answer, assuming he was calling back to question me about my statement the previous afternoon. I'm not sure what made me ultimately decide to accept the call, but I needn't have worried. He was clearly in a rush, nearly panting, and I could hear footsteps, loud ones, as if he were running.

"They have a verdict," he said between breaths. "They must have needed to sleep on it, because they notified the bailiff within five minutes of entering the jury room this morning. I'm on my way to meet Lena at the complex now."

So here it was, then. "Do I have time to get there?" Memphis was nearly an hour away.

"You have forty-five minutes."

I dressed quickly, zipping my hygiene bag with a sense of finality before loading the car with my few belongings. After giving the house a final walk-through to close and lock windows, I stepped onto the porch for the last time, locked the door behind me, and placed the key under a loose brick in the front planter, as Mrs. Myers and I had prearranged.

It was a gorgeous day outside, the sky a deep, cloudless blue the way it sometimes is in September. I stood for just a moment enjoying the breeze, listening to the chirp of birds, the rustling of a fox squirrel in leaves under the pecan tree. *Rusty*, I remembered. Years ago, when Lena was maybe six or seven, a similar squirrel had frequented that same spot. We'd watched for him every afternoon after school, Lena, Callie, and I, all three of us shrieking with excitement when he appeared.

Look at his fur, Lena. Isn't he pretty?

He's rusty, she'd said, and so he was named.

Then one day Mr. Carter's beagle, Wesley, jumped the fence, and Rusty was no more. Callie saw it happen, but of course she couldn't tell us. What she did do was scream, loudly, piercingly, launching her body from side to side with enough force to knock her wheelchair over. We'd come running, my mother and I, setting the chair upright with Callie still strapped in the seat, frantically searching her body for injuries, begging her to tell us what was wrong. It was I who followed her line of vision and saw. I ran outside, yelling and waving my arms until Wesley dropped the squirrel and ran up to me, tail wagging, as if to say, "Look what I did! Aren't I a good boy?" I buried Rusty behind the tool shed before Lena could see him. As far as I know, she still believes he moved away for the winter.

The current squirrel jumped when I slammed my car trunk, running up the tree and chattering angrily from the end of a branch two feet above my head. "You can have it," I said to him softly. "It's all yours." My promise didn't seem to ease his consternation; his furious squeaks and chirps followed me into my car, the last sounds I'd ever hear from that farm, and perhaps the most fitting.

I drove away without looking back.

She was nervous. She hid it well, but I knew. It was evident in the way she sat, spine straight, hands in lap, eyes looking straight ahead. This posture from a woman who'd slouched her way through life, seeming to melt into every surface upon which she sat. From my seat behind her, I could see her breathing, her shoulders rising and falling more slowly than was natural as she worked to keep herself calm. Had I been close enough, I might have reached over the rail to place a hand on her shoulder. I might have given it a little squeeze, a small gesture of comfort to ease her anxiety.

But I was too far away.

Just then, Brian turned and saw me, lifting his chin slightly in greeting. He leaned toward Lena, encircling her shoulders with his arm and bending close to whisper in her ear. Her shoulders relaxed slightly, the teeniest bit, and she turned to see me. *Thank you*, she mouthed silently before turning back to Brian.

Things happened quickly after that. The judge entered and ordered the jury to be brought into the courtroom. I watched Lena as they filed in, but she kept her head straight, eyes forward. Brian, on the other hand, watched them closely, his expression inscrutable, and I wondered what he was seeing and if it gave him hope. All I saw were twelve tired-looking people, a mix of old and young, black and white, men and women, all of whom seemed to studiously avoid making eye contact with anyone in the courtroom.

Someone, a court clerk of some sort, I supposed, instructed the jurors to answer as their names were called. One by one, they answered with, "Here," as if they were reluctant students answering roll call the first day of school.

"How say you?" the clerk asked, and for the smallest fraction of time, there was utter silence in the courtroom. I could hear my heart beating, and when I listened closely, thought I could hear Lena's, too, though that can't have been possible. Brian reached for her hand, and she twined her fingers through his, clinging with enough force to turn her fingertips white. Thus anchored, she stood, trembling, head bowed, and waited.

"We the jury, find the defendant, Lena Suzette Reynolds, not guilty."

There was a collective gasp. Lena swayed; Brian caught her. The judge called for order.

And I? I stood and walked down the center aisle, pushed open the heavy double doors, and shoved my way past scrambling reporters and curious townsfolk. Stepping outside into the parking lot, I removed my shoes and my jacket, untucked my blouse, and pulled the pins from my hair. The sun was warm, but not too hot. I lowered the windows and turned up the radio before merging onto I-40, leaving Memphis behind for good.

Chapter 37: Brian Stone
November, 2016

"IT WASN'T BLOOD Patty Sue saw," Lena says, her voice cutting through the fog of my sleep. "I remember now. Brian? Do you hear me?"

I sit up, rubbing the sleep out of my eyes, squinting to see Lena's silhouette in the doorway. Backlit by the light from the hall, she almost looks like an angel, albeit one with a slightly crooked halo. The thought makes me smile.

"What are you talking about, Lena? It's three o'clock in the morning."

"I know, and I'm sorry. But I had another dream, and I wanted to tell you about it before I forget."

"Come sit." I move over and pat the bed beside me, arranging a layer of pillows against the headboard. "Tell me all your dreams, little girl."

"Stop it," she says, swatting at me. "This is serious."

"Now you're the serious one. Who'd have ever thought?"

"Very funny." She settles in beside me and rests her head on my shoulder, pulling the quilt up and hugging it to her chest.

"Tell me about this dream."

A deep sigh. "I was walking," she says, "down Bucktail Road. It was dark."

"Go on."

"The world keeps tilting, and I fall down over and over again. I hold my arms out, hands in front of me, trying to get my balance, and see I'm covered with mud. My hands, arms, knees. I'm walking in a ditch filled with muck. It's hard to walk through; my legs keep buckling. I see headlights coming toward me. Two, four, six. I'm so dizzy, I can't tell. When they get closer they merge back into two, and someone honks at me. It scares me. The car flies past, and I stumble and fall again. I crawl out of the ditch—I'm literally dragging myself out of it—to try and stand, but this time I can't regain my footing. I'm falling, rolling down a small hill. I land on something soft. Sand. I'm so tired. I need to get up, I think, so I can go home. But where is home? Maybe I *am* home. I feel as if I am. I feel as if my parents are there, and Callie, and Rebecca, too. I close my eyes to sleep."

"And then what?" I ask softly. She speaks as if she's in a trance, and I don't want to break it.

"Then I'm lying on my back in the spot down by the river where I used to meet Rebecca when she came looking for me. My pants are around my ankles, and … Well, you know the rest."

We sit in silence and I stroke her hair until I hear her breathing deepen. Gently, I remove my arm from around her shoulders and adjust the pillows behind her. Leaving her to my bed, I lift my robe from the back of the door and tiptoe down the hallway, careful not to step on any creaking boards. The cabin is old, making its age known in a series of creaks and sighs as it settles for the night. That's one of the many things I love about it.

I step onto the porch, closing the door softly behind me. The moon is full, a perfect backdrop to bare branches stretching up toward the sky. I sit on the swing, setting it in motion with one foot, Anna's laughter echoing in my head. *You're such a kid, Brian. You're going to swing it right off the chains.* I still miss them; I suppose I always will. Thankfully, the good memories are finally replacing the bad ones. The wind kicks up, cold fingers working their way through my robe, and I shiver, but it's the delicious kind of shiver experienced when warmth is just a step away.

I enjoy this time with Lena. It took her a while to settle in, to trust me not to expect something in return. This isn't the first time she's come to me for comfort in the middle of the night, and it's not the first time I've tucked her safely into my bed, and—once she's sleeping—gone alone to finish out the night in hers. This is all I want from her, this kinship. What Lena doesn't understand is that she pays me back by her very presence. This is not a role she's used to filling, and it's a difficult one for her to accept. She answers a need in me, and I like to think I do the same for her. We're both in a limbo of sorts, a safe, comforting place between times, but that's okay. That's fine for now. I'm learning to heal, and I think she is, too.

Object Relations Theory. I hear Anna in my head again. A warm spring day, the smell of coffee. A lazy morning with my two best friends. *The belief that your ego, your* self, *only exists in relation to something else*, Anna is saying, *or* someone *else.*

If this so-called theory is right, I'd responded, *wouldn't that mean our lives are nothing more than a reaction to whatever—or whomever—we choose to keep around us? If that's the case, we'd better be really careful with our choices, hadn't we?*

"I'm being careful, Anna," I whisper into the darkness. "I'm making the right choices." Ghost-Anna rolls her eyes at me before drifting away on the wind, leaving me alone with my thoughts.

I've been nursing one particular thought for some time, probably since before the trial ended. It didn't appear all at once, which makes tracking it difficult. Instead, it faded in slowly, blurred around the edges, cloudy in the middle, a little more color added each day until it snapped into focus tonight, accompanied by the sound of Lena's voice as she recounted her dream.

All I have is a thought, mind you, and I'll need more than that.

For the first time in my life, I'm almost free, Rebecca had said.

Almost.

I wonder what will happen if she decides she's not quite free enough.

I wonder when Lena will remember everything.

I wonder how much danger she's in while we wait.

Chapter 38: Rebecca
November, 2016

LET ME TELL you a story. Settle in, get comfortable. Pour yourself a drink and listen up.

Once upon a time, there was a middle-aged woman named Rebecca. She wasn't the fairest in the land, but she wasn't too shabby for her age. She had long dark hair threaded with gray, and wide-set blue eyes behind tortoise-shell bifocals, and although she'd been teased for being skinny throughout her childhood, she'd come to appreciate the long lankiness of her body, the hard angles having developed soft curves over the years.

She no longer received whistles and cat calls from young men brimming with testosterone, but older men, such as Marco from the local fish stand, or Juan from the lobby of her hotel, still cast appreciative glances her way when she walked by, especially if she wore her black dress, the one with soft cotton folds that clung to a body still shapely and toned.

She was enough of a feminist to know she should feel offended by those looks.

But she didn't.

She felt young and free and pretty—and just sexy enough to put a little extra sway in her step.

This Rebecca had no friends, keeping her distance, but that was okay. That was just fine. She'd had a lifetime of living for other people.

Now, Rebecca lived for herself.

Playa Paraiso is gorgeous this time of year. I spend my days browsing local shops, reading, sometimes writing. I dream of publishing a memoir someday, but as interesting as my story may be, that can obviously never happen.

I spend my evenings walking the beach and thinking.

It all began that warm spring Saturday, the day I found my father under the elm tree. *Your mother is sick,* he'd said. *I'm going to need some help.* I'd known the time would come, of course. I'd been groomed for it all my life. I'd move home and care for my mother and Callie. After my mother's death, I'd care for Callie and my father. Beyond that was a void; I couldn't see anything else. I'd never attempted to see anything else, immobilized by fear. What if the unknown proved to be worse than the known?

Still, I think it could have been okay. Had that been the extent of our conversation, I'd have said my goodbyes and driven the four hours back to my apartment to shower and collapse, exhausted but at the same time relieved to be home. I may have called Brenda to complain, and she'd have commiserated with me. She'd have made it funny somehow; Brenda was like that. She'd have mocked my dad's narcissism in a way that removed the sting for me, if not for him. She'd have comforted me with promises of weekend visits and overnights at the farm, painting a storybook picture of hiking through wildflower fields and sipping homemade apple cider. I'd have believed her, whether she meant it or not, because I was desperate to believe.

But that hadn't been the end of my conversation with my father, because he'd had a question for me.

Was I a bad father?

I'd sorted through memories, searching for good ones, for proof our home hadn't been as joyless as it seemed. And then I'd lied, because as we both knew, he didn't ask in order to receive an honest answer; he asked in order to receive comfort. Maybe on a different day, a day during which I hadn't spent hours completing a list of chores I'd end up repeating the next Saturday, a day on which I hadn't been so overwhelmed, on which I didn't feel as if I were drowning in the futility of it all … maybe on a day like that, I would have answered honestly. Or maybe not. It's impossible to know.

What I *do* know is that my little mental journey back through time made one thing crystal clear: I could not move back there. I could not be in that home, with those people, living that life. I'd die first. I'd kill myself.

Or…

At first I dismissed the idea out of hand, ashamed of myself for even having such a thought, but no matter how many times I batted it away, it always wormed its way back in. I'd find myself fantasizing at my station, plotting details while simultaneously counting rivets and weighing boxes.

The thing is, the more I considered it, the easier it seemed to do. Not just the mental acceptance of it, but the *mechanics* of it, almost as if the universe were granting me the opportunity, lining up the tools I needed, damn near placing them in my hands.

Willie G. cemented that belief. He approached me that very next weekend, almost as if he'd been summoned. I'd just finished the larger areas with the riding mower and was struggling to start the push mower. The damn thing was at least ten years old and notoriously difficult to start. I'd yanked the cord for the eighth or ninth time without luck before taking a break to swear and catch my breath. "Let me get that for you," Willie G. had said with his toothless smile. I hadn't even known he was there until that moment, when I saw him walking toward me with an axe in one hand, and a handsaw in the other.

"I'd appreciate it," I said. "Just give me a minute to cool off first." I leaned back against the tool shed, under the awning, taking care not to disturb the wasps busily building a nest in an upper corner. "It's hot as hell out here today."

"It is that," he said, leaning the axe against the shed and joining me under the awning. "Might have to go fishing when I'm done here, catch me some blues, drink a cold one, maybe two." He smiled again and nudged me with his elbow, clearly flirting.

"Where do you fish?" I asked, not really caring, but being silent with Willie G. was even more awkward than talking with him. I angled away from both his bony elbow and his stench.

"The Mississippi," he said, jerking his chin in the general direction. "There's some big boys in that river. Caught me one a year or two ago must have weighed fifty pounds."

I didn't half believe him, but I went along with it. Having him start that damn mower for me was worth the price of humoring him for a minute. "Where do you fish it?"

"Got a trailer down there, right where the road drops off. Got an aluminum boat. No motor, so you have to be careful in the currents, but I've never had a problem. Not one I couldn't handle, anyway." He winked, and I struggled to keep my expression friendly while I let his words sink in. *Right where the road drops off.*

Willie G. lived down in the bottoms.

Where Lena also lived.

You can see where I'm going with this.

I'll spare you the worst of the details, but let's just say after a few conversations with Willie G., I paid my family a surprise visit the evening of July 13, 2015. No one knew I was going to the farm, not my family, not my coworkers. Not even Willie G. I'd put in a full day of work, smoked a cigarette with Brenda in the parking lot, waved goodbye, and bypassed my apartment, making damn good time. I arrived at the farm just after 7:00 p.m.

I parked around back under the oaks, pushing the car door softly closed instead of slamming it. I stripped off my clothes before creeping to the tool shed, ducking through shadows. I knew where everything was: axe, gloves, my father's rubber waders. When I was ready, I rang the front doorbell.

"Rebecca, what in the world—"

Did as much as any boy could have done, and probably stronger than half of them, my father had said. I still was, even at my age. A lifetime of farm work will do that for a woman.

One down. Two to go.

What happened with Callie was an accident. I would have never wanted to make Callie suffer, but I was rattled; she'd seen what had happened to our mother and was doing that screaming thing she does—did—slamming her body around in the chair, in danger of tipping it over. In my hurry to get to her I tripped; my aim was off. I delivered mercy and ended her pain as quickly as I could.

I would never deliberately make Callie suffer.

No matter how much of a monster you think me to be, you need to believe this.

The noise brought my father, of course. I heard him coming from the bedroom, where he'd been watching television, the volume turned high enough to rupture an eardrum. His work boots thudded on the wooden floor and, knowing the house as I did, I counted his steps. Five, six, seven …

"What the hell is going on—"

… eight.

My father was a big man. He didn't make it easy for me, which meant I couldn't make it easy for him.

I hosed off outside and threw the axe, gloves, and waders into the back of Daddy's farm truck. I dressed and then carefully let myself in through the back door. I went through the kitchen, avoiding the living room. It pained me to see them in that state.

It truly did.

Retrieving the safe from Daddy's office, I went back outside and hefted it over the tailgate, wincing at the noise it made when it fell.

Then I headed for the bottoms.

I couldn't very well kill Lena, because that would have been too obvious, but there were other ways to get rid of her. Or so I'd thought. Things didn't work out exactly as I'd planned.

For example, I hadn't planned on Willie G. freaking out on me. I'd bet—wrongly, as it turned out—a little flirting and a lot of money would keep him in check. Daddy had $1,000 in the safe, and that's what I offered Willie G. to drug Lena and bring her to me. He was supposed to put her in his aluminum boat and row a mile upriver, where I'd pick her up and he'd go off to do whatever it is bottom-dwellers do under cover of darkness. But he changed the plan on me.

"Here she is," he'd said, stashing his boat in the brush before gently picking Lena up and placing her body into the truck's bed. "Do you have the money?"

"Do you have the drugs? I don't need her waking up until I'm finished with her."

He reached through the passenger window to hand me two vials, and I handed over the final wad of hundreds. Our deal complete, I put the truck in drive, but he opened the door before I could leave.

"I don't know what you're planning to do with her, but I'm going with you."

"You're out of your mind," I'd responded. "That's not our deal." I stomped on the gas, a mistake, as it turned out, because for a few seconds my tires simply spun in the sand, giving Willie G. enough time to dive into the passenger seat and slam the door shut.

"What the hell, Willie?"

"I don't trust you."

"I gave you your money."

"I don't trust you with Lena."

I laughed. "You're a strange guardian angel, Willie G. For a thousand dollars, you drugged my sister half to death."

"She'll wake up," he said. "She'll be fine, but I can't just let you take her. I've thought about this all day. I've done a lot of bad things in my life, stealing is one of them, but I can't just hand over an unconscious woman."

There wasn't much I could do. I certainly couldn't wrestle him out of the truck. I'd figure it out later; I'd come too far to stop now.

"Keep an eye on Lena," I instructed as I pulled back onto Bucktail Road, "and when we get to the house, you wait outside."

He didn't, of course, which was how Lena ended up acquitted, and Willie G. ended up dead. Collateral damage, as they say. All I'd needed was Lena's handprints, something to prove she was there in order to lead the police to her. Everyone knew Lena's history with our parents. The idea she may have killed them and stolen their safe certainly wasn't a stretch.

Had Willie G. not intervened I'd have been back at the river in under an hour, the safe, gloves, axe, and waders resting on the river bottom with Adonis, and Lena sleeping it off in the bushes beside Bucktail Road. As it turned out, I'd had to use the last two vials on Willie G. He'd tried to run for it, jumping into Daddy's farm truck, not realizing the keys were in my pocket. It's not easy to load a comatose man into a boat in the middle of the night. It's even harder to dump him out, but I managed, though I damn near flipped the boat in the process. Had it not been for the safe awaiting its turn, holding the boat steady, I'd have probably drowned right alongside Willie.

By the time I'd retrieved my car and driven home, it was nearly 5:00 a.m. I showered and dressed, downed three cups of coffee, and went to work, pulling into the lot at 6:55, right behind Brenda. Every nerve, every muscle and fiber in my body screamed in agony, but I made it through the day. I made it all week, just as I always do, until it was time to go back to the farm Saturday and do my chores.

That's when I stumbled across the mutilated bodies of my parents and younger sister.

See how that worked?

It's true things didn't work out exactly as I'd expected. I'd expected Lena to be convicted. I hadn't realized Willie G.'s hat was still in Daddy's truck. I also hadn't realized he'd pissed himself during our ride back to the bottoms. It was dark, after all, and Willie G. always stank. I'd initially argued with Brian, trying to force blame back to Lena, but he'd held steady. It was curious, to me, how much he believed in Lena. When we found out Daddy had fired Willie G., giving him motive, there was no convincing anyone otherwise.

Still, I'm free, and that's what matters.

I'm free, and the sunset is gorgeous.

I'm free, and the breeze is fresh, smelling of salt and sand, caressing my face, making me dream of far-away places.

I'm free, and the gentle waves lapping at my feet are warm; the foam tickles my heels.

I'm free, and the seagulls overhead swoop and dive as if in celebration.

I'm free.

And so is Lena.

Finish your chores, Daddy had always said, but I hadn't.

Not quite yet.

Book Club Discussion Starters

Upon stumbling over the bodies of her parents and sister, Rebecca wonders where her surviving sister is and says, "My third [thought] was to wonder how much time we had before her arrest. This is important, this third thought of mine. If you stick with my story, you'll understand why." Why would Rebecca have wondered when her sister would be arrested?

When Lena crashed the stage at the Miss Teen Soybean pageant and was disowned by her father, she turned to the "stupidly hopeful Miss Teen Soybeans arranged like so many colorful flower stalks behind him and told them to run while they still could. I thought it was damned good advice, myself, but apparently he didn't agree." Why might Lena have thought this "damned good advice" to give the young girls? Do you agree?

When Rebecca remembers her early childhood, when she worked the farm with her father, she remembers "A *good* kind of quiet." Given her family dynamics, what do you think she means by this?

The day Rebecca sat with her father under the elm tree and learned her mother was sick, she worked to pull up a dandelion plant, thinking, "Best to get rid of it while it was alive; otherwise, the seeds would spread and make more work for me." In hindsight, what else might Rebecca have been thinking in that moment?

Rebecca recounts an incident in which her father forced her to have lunch with an elderly man who "…

pull[ed] me onto his lap, the hardness against my bottom something I didn't comprehend until later." She remembers that Lena, age seven at the time, was also forced to have lunch with the man. She then says, "I wondered if, prostituting herself down on that riverbank, Lena also remembered." What parallel is Rebecca drawing between their father forcing them to visit the elderly man, and Lena "prostituting herself" down in the bottoms?

At one point Rebecca says about Lena, "… while I *hadn't* been the one to hurt her, she *had* been the one to hurt me." Is this an accurate statement?

Lena notes, "The Lower Mississippi is notoriously fickle, full of shifting currents and powerful whirlpools." Why is Lena so drawn to the river?

Lena asks, "What does it say about me that *raped* wasn't the first word that came to mind when I regained consciousness on that riverbank, covered with flies, my knees splayed open?" What do we learn about Lena from this statement?

Speaking of his time with Lena after the trial, Brian says, "We're both in a limbo of sorts, a safe, comforting place between times, but that's okay." What does he mean by this?

Rebecca says, "I would never deliberately make Callie suffer. No matter how much of a monster you think me to be, you need to believe this." Do you believe her? Why or why not?

More Books by Melinda Clayton

The Tennessee Delta Series
Blessed Are the Wholly Broken, Book 1

The Cedar Hollow Series
Appalachian Justice, Book 1
Return to Crutcher Mountain, Book 2
Entangled Thorns, Book 3
Shadow Days, Book 4

Making Amends

About the Author

Melinda Clayton has published numerous articles and short stories in various print and online magazines. In addition to writing, she has an Ed.D. in Special Education Administration and is a licensed psychotherapist in the states of Florida and Colorado.

For news about Melinda, you can visit her website at www.melindaclayton.net or sign up for the Thomas-Jacob Publishing, LLC newsletter at www.thomas-jacobpublishing.com to learn about sales, freebies, new releases and other events.